LOVE ON THE MOOR

Her career and London life in ruins, Daisy Weston flees to the West country, buys her dream cottage in a remote moorland village and starts to build an organic herb business. When unexpected and menacing events begin to cloud the rural idyll, she suspects Jack Hawksworth, a powerful local landowner. But, unknown to Daisy, there are more sinister interests intent on removing her from the cottage as she discovers rural life is far more dangerous than its tranquil beauty suggests.

Books should be returned on or before the
last date stamped below

2 9 FEB 2016

29 DEC 2004

1 5 APR 2008   30. JAN 12.

1 6 JUN 2008   28. SEP 12

2 0 JAN 2005

1 8 JUL 2008   15. MAY 13.

2 7 AUG 2008

2 1 FEB 2005   2 6 JAN 2009

10 MAR 2005   − 5 MAY 2009

1 0 MAY 2005   2 0 AUG 2009   2 6 NOV 2015   N°35

2 4 JUN 2005   12. AUG 10.   18/1/16

1 9 AUG 2005   1 5 FEB 2016

MK

JOYCE JOHNSON

LOVE ON
THE MOOR

Complete and Unabridged

LINFORD
Leicester

First published in Great Britain in 2001

First Linford Edition
published 2004

Johnson, Joyce,
Love on the
moor / Joyce
Johnson

British Library CIP Data

Johnson, Joyce
Love on the moor.— ROM LP
Large print ed.—
Linford romance library
1489417
1. Love stories
2. Large type books
I. Title
823.9′14 [F]

ISBN 1–84395–532–6

Published by
F. A. Thorpe (Publishing)
Anstey, Leicestershire

Set by Words & Graphics Ltd.
Anstey, Leicestershire
Printed and bound in Great Britain by
T. J. International Ltd., Padstow, Cornwall

This book is printed on acid-free paper

1

Daisy Weston braked sharply enough to raise an irate honking from the flashy car that had been on her tail for the past few miles. Getting out of London on a late Friday afternoon had been nightmare enough, added to that, she hadn't driven for weeks and the car itself was unfamiliar. She'd been so busy nervously watching the car in her rear mirror she nearly missed the slip road into the service station.

Now she entered it far too fast, very nearly crashing into the car ahead. The driver ahead appeared not to have noticed how closely she'd come to crashing into him and the other car driver hadn't followed her to give her a blast of road rage.

She let out a breath and eased her car very slowly towards the hotel at the rear of the carpark and switched off the ignition. She was shaking, ridiculous, simply because an impatient motorist had honked her. It happened all the time in London and it had never bothered her, battling with the rest of them for road space. But that was before . . .

'No,' she said aloud. 'No more dwelling in the past,' she'd promised Aunt Lucy.

The dashboard clock registered seven o'clock, still plenty of daylight but she was too tired to carry on. It had been a strain driving again and this travel lodge chain hotel suited her perfectly. Tucked away behind the restaurant and petrol pumps it was faceless and anonymous, perfect cover.

These days, Daisy tended to avoid people's eyes but the receptionist didn't even look up from her computer screen to Daisy's enquiry about a room, replying automatically.

'Single? Just the one night? How do you want to pay?'

'Single, one night, credit card.'

The girl's fingers whizzed over the keys then handed Daisy a numbered strip of plastic.

'Down the corridor, turn left. Morning paper?'

'No!'

'Oh.'

The girl looked startled by the force of Daisy's response.

'Sorry, but I'll be leaving too early. Thanks.'

The receptionist shrugged and swivelled back to the computer. Daisy pulled her heavy case along the silent corridor. She should have packed a smaller overnight bag but her decision had been swift and sudden. But for Aunt Lucy's phone call the previous night she would still be moping and skulking in her small, expensive rented studio flat in South London, too scared even to go to the corner shop.

She couldn't afford to have the phone connected but irrationally she'd kept her mobile, a necessity in the old life, rarely used now. People had called at first but she had been unresponsive and gradually the calls had dwindled away to those from her parents and aunt. Aunt Lucy's call last night had made her jump and she nearly left it unanswered but force of habit prevailed.

'Hello.'

She was tentative, holding the instrument away from her.

'Daisy? Is that you? Do speak up. What are you doing right now?'

'Oh . . . just . . . um . . . '

'Nothing, I warrant. Just sitting in that horrid bedsit staring out of the window at equally horrid buildings opposite, all chopped up into units for the lost and lonely.'

'It's not as bad as that. You make it sound like a prison. It's a . . . well, it's a base.'

'Oho,' Lucy Weston pounced, 'a base. Oh, sure, if you were working you wouldn't even notice but now . . . '

'Now I'm out of a job,' Daisy interrupted bitterly.

'I didn't call to go over that. That's in the past, over and done with.'

'It isn't. I can't work and it's unfair.'

'Oh, stop it, Daisy. You've been drowning in self pity long enough. I've waited for you to come to your senses but there's no sign of that. I have to say I'm disappointed. I thought you had more spunk. You used to have lots of it . . . no, don't interrupt, listen to me. You've got to pick yourself up, start working.'

'I'll never get a job in medicine now.'

The words burst out of Daisy.

'Sh, child. Medicine isn't the only profession in this life. In any case, it was Edward who pushed you in that direction in the first place.'

'Dad thought it was the right thing for me.'

'Look I don't want to talk about my brother this evening. It's you I'm concerned about. Forget medicine. Look around you at all the other options, Daisy. What about all those e.dot.com. things, you know in computers? Millionaires overnight! I've been using the internet. Fascinating.'

'You're on the internet?'

''Course I am. I'm not ready for the old folks' home yet, as you'd know if you'd lift yourself out of this miserable state you're in.'

'But you don't like new technology.'

'I disapprove of all these people going around with machines clamped to their ears jabbering trivia at each other all day. The internet's different, and I can't be living in the past like you. Now, I just want you to listen carefully.'

'I am.'

'So you realise you've got to do something?'

'I suppose.'

Daisy flicked on the television and pressed mute — something to watch while Aunt Lucy lectured her. This wasn't like her favourite aunt. She'd been one of the few who'd avoided the what-you-should-do approach. From the outset she'd been briskly sympathetic, listened to Daisy's side of things and advised a complete change of scene, exactly as she was doing now.

'But I can't just up and leave and tour the country looking for work, not on benefit. I can just afford to hang on here.'

'For what?' Lucy persisted.

Daisy gave a mental shrug and watched the screen, an old film. She'd watched a lot of old films lately. They passed the time. Aunt Lucy's angry voice snapped her attention back to the phone.

' . . . almost ashamed of you. This is a last chance and if you don't take it I'll . . . I'll disinherit you and never speak to you again, ever.'

'Aunt Lucy, don't. I couldn't bear that, not speak to you again, I mean.'

'Well then, do as I tell you, and I'm telling, not asking. Pack up tonight, leave that scabby old bedsit and go, right away, this minute.'

'How can I?' Daisy almost wailed. 'I've five pounds to last the week and

I'm certainly not asking Dad for any money.'

'Quite right, but no need to. Not your problem. You know all my money comes to you when I'm dead?'

'Don't.'

'Oh, I'm not going yet, dear, but I've made some wise investments which have paid off pretty handsomely and I'm releasing a wodge of cash for you to use now when you're most in need of it. It'll be transferred to your bank account, and I've spoken to the man at your garage you used to use. He can have a car ready for you right away, so pick up your bits and pieces, wash your hair or whatever and just go.'

Daisy could already feel the panic fluttering in her throat.

'I can't, really.'

'Why not?'

How could she explain the panics, the sweats which overcame her before she even set foot in the street?

'I just can't, that's all.'

There was a long silence, such a sad,

resigned silence Daisy could see her aunt's face sag with disappointment and it tore at her heart.

'Well, then, so be it.'

The fire had gone out of Lucy Weston and her soft sigh indicated defeat.

Daisy looked out of the window. There were lots of people on the street, singly, in pairs or groups, all confidently going about their business, just as she, Daisy Weston, used to, and surely would again when she'd snapped out of this deadly lethargy. But wasn't Aunt Lucy throwing her just the lifeline she needed? And if she didn't take it she knew she'd drown. She put a hand on her heart and took a deep breath.

'OK, Aunt Lucy, I accept, but I'd prefer the money as a loan.'

The soft sigh became a hiss of triumph.

'Good girl, Daisy.'

It sounded as though she'd brought her pet spaniel to heel and Daisy giggled, her first hint of laughter for months.

'No need. I'm talking big money. Buy a house, not in London of course, far too expensive, dreadful value for money, but maybe somewhere in the country. Set up a business perhaps. I'll get on to your garage first thing, transfer the money now.'

'You'd do all this just to make me . . . ' Daisy's voice choked.

'Now, now, you know me, always looking for a project. You're it at the moment, my mission. Don't let me down. So, get moving. No time to waste.'

'I won't let you down. I promise.'

After the phone call Daisy had run down the stairs out into the street to the corner shop where she startled Mrs Patel with a cheerful greeting and bought a bottle of white wine and a pizza.

'Goodness me,' Mrs Patel said to her husband, 'whatever's been ailing that girl seems to have vanished. That's the

10

first time I've seen her smile since she's been here. I wonder what her problem was.'

Mrs Patel smiled at her next customer and forgot about Daisy.

All Daisy's problems just then were purely practical. She drank her wine, ate her pizza and made a list, galvanised at last into a purpose, short term admittedly but better than lying in bed half the day and staring out of the window or watching old films.

Before she packed her lap-top she checked her e-mail for the first time in days. One or two were from friends worried about her, why she didn't contact them, where was she living now, what plans had she made? One was from the hospital curtly reminding her she still held a locker key and could she return it and remove any belongings from the premises? She deleted the lot. She'd pick up the threads later. For now she wanted to sever all connections with that part of her life which had brought her nothing but sadness and heartache.

At last she was done, the place cleaned, empty of any trace of her brief stay. There was one more task she'd put off until last, the one thing she really didn't want to do but she had to do it. Her mother would worry otherwise. She dialled her parents' number and listened to the ringing tone praying her father wouldn't pick up the phone. To her relief the answerphone kicked in.

'Uh, hi, Dad, Mum. Just to tell you I'm moving out, leaving London. I'll call again as soon as I reach wherever.'

She switched off the phone and dropped it as though it was red hot, her palms clammy, but that was that. On her way, fresh start, and tomorrow night she could be anywhere. A faint excitement trickled through her veins and for the first time in months Daisy Weston went to bed and slept dreamlessly until morning.

Now, as soon as she was settled in the hotel room she dialled for an outside line.

'Aunt Lucy? Daisy.'

'Where are you?'

'Don't panic. I'm out of London, travelling westwards. I didn't leave until late afternoon. I had to hand over the key. The landlord was really nice, gave me my deposit back straight away and waived notice.'

'People are decent on the whole. Don't lose sight of that, Daisy.'

'That's difficult just yet.'

'You'll get there. Keep me posted. Car all right?'

'Great. Thanks. For the first time since my world collapsed I feel alive.'

'Good girl. You're very welcome.'

The novelty of the situation kept Daisy going over the next few days. She stopped at Bristol, then Bath, but the crowded streets and endless traffic oppressed her. It was too similar to London, claustrophobic and not what she was looking for though she was hard put to know exactly what she was looking for. When she found it, she hoped she'd know.

Instinctively she headed deeper into the West Country avoiding motorways then dual carriageways, always taking minor roads and lanes through tiny, sleepy villages and hamlets, crossing moorland, frequently going round in circles and coming back to the same landmark or village.

One such village caught her attention, its one street backed by moorland. There was a small post office and store, a straggle of cottages and an inn set back from the road, its rough stone walls and thatched roof blending perfectly with its surroundings. It had the oddest name — The Skittish Pony.

It was late afternoon, a golden mellow day, blue skies, picture postcard setting, quiet, peaceful. Daisy pushed open the heavy wooden door of The Skittish Pony and stooped to avoid the low-beamed entrance. It was dark and cool. She blinked to adjust her eyes from the brightness outside. A large man behind the bar looked startled at her request for a room and dinner.

'What, tonight?' he asked in astonishment.

'Yes, if you're open.'

There was no-one else in the room or anywhere else she could see.

'Oh, aye, sure, but 'tis, well, it's not the main season yet.'

'But it's midsummer.'

'Yes, but we're off the main tourist route. Mainly fishing folk, at weekends. There's a much bigger village ten miles along, one or two hotels there. You're not a tourist, are you?'

Daisy was taken back by his scrutiny.

'Sort of. No, not really, but sort of a holiday.'

He obviously didn't find her answer very satisfactory. Still watching her, her jerked his head towards the back and called out, 'Martha.'

Daisy stood awkwardly by the bar. Something odd here, perhaps best to walk out, but she liked the place. It was vastly different from London pubs.

'Early yet,' the man said, 'liven up later. Mebbe.'

'I don't need livening up. I like the quiet, but if it's too much trouble . . . '

'No, that's what we're here for. Martha,' he roared as a small, plump woman materialised from the shadows behind the bar.

'No need to yell, Bob. I'm not deaf.'

She smiled at Daisy.

'Young lady would like a room tonight, supper, too,' Bob said more quietly but doubtfully.

'Well, of course. Don't just stand there, take . . . '

She looked enquiringly at Daisy.

'Er, Weston, Daisy Weston.'

'Take Miss Weston's bags up to number four. It's a lovely, quiet room at the back, view over the moors, en suite, TV. What time will you be wanting dinner?'

'Whenever's convenient. I'd like to go for a walk first. I've been travelling.'

'Come far?' Bob asked quickly.

Daisy hesitated.

'Bristol.'

'Not so far to Bristol. I thought you said travelling.'

'Bob, leave Miss Weston be. It's none of our business.'

'I'm sorry . . . I mean . . . '

Daisy floundered, caught up again between the misery of anxiety and paranoia. How could these people know about her and why should they care? Anyway, she'd already decided it was high time to stop being so self absorbed.

'I've come from London actually,' she said firmly, 'via Bristol.'

'Ah, well, that answers the case,' Bob said enigmatically as he picked up her bag and trudged towards the staircase.

Martha rolled her eyes heavenwards.

'Don't mind him,' she said. 'You go for your walk. Take the road behind here, bear right, it'll take you to the river. Lovely there this time of day.'

★   ★   ★

Daisy sat with her back against a huge, sun-warmed granite boulder watching the sun's last golden rays dapple the stream, swishing and swirling over pebbles and against rocks. Her body relaxed, her eyes closed. This was the place to be, not in some cramped bedsit with the noisy lives of a dozen other inmates crowding in on her.

It should be possible in such a place to recover and rebuild her life away from cities and people. This was a good place, she felt. Walking to the water's edge she crouched down to scoop up the clear crystal water in her hands. Suddenly she jerked back on her heels as a rapid succession of cracks shattered the peaceful tranquillity.

It sounded like gunfire, quite near. Standing up she looked around, unsure of her bearings. More shots, much nearer. What direction had she come from? She'd wandered too far from the inn. In a panic, she struck out away from the stream and the gunfire and walked rapidly towards a thick clump of trees which looked vaguely familiar. More shots, even nearer, and she thought she heard shouting. Fear rose in her throat as she ran stumbling over the uneven ground, her breath rasping sharply.

'Hoy, you, stop,' a man's voice, rough and hostile, shouted.

Faster and faster she sped towards the trees, terror giving her speed, until she finally plunged through a dense patch of scrub and gorse into the shelter of a copse. Bent double with a crippling stitch she tried to still her breath. No sound. She waited for what seemed hours, minutes in reality, then far in the distance she heard a long, low whistle and a dog barking.

What a fool. It was simply a man out with his dog, maybe shooting rabbits or crows. Feeling utterly stupid she stood up. There wasn't a soul in sight. Maybe she'd even imagined the whole thing. She'd been out of the world too long. Aunt Lucy was quite right, it was time to pull herself together, get on with her life and stop imagining life was about to deal her more crippling body blows.

Now she remembered approaching that copse from the left, the inn was over to the right, straight back across the moor. Pulling her shoulders back she set off at a brisk pace hoping she was travelling in the right direction.

2

It was an odd sensation, rediscovering the pleasure of hunger pangs about to be satisfied. Daisy was the only person in the dining end of the long bar. Perfect, all the better to enjoy Martha's deliciously-smelling pie.

'Bit of this and that pie,' she announced as she set a plate, the pie and a heaped tureen of vegetables in front of Daisy later that evening. 'All the veggies home grown,' she added. 'For all his faults Bob can coax a mountain of produce from his plot round the back.'

She pulled the cork of a bottle of wine.

'Compliments of the house,' she said, eyeing Daisy shrewdly. 'Tell me to mind my own business if you want but you look as though you've been ill.'

Daisy watched the dark red wine slip

from bottle to glass.

'I have,' she said decisively, 'but do you know I feel recovery setting in and maybe in this place . . . '

'A few days here would be good. Lovely air, walks, peace and quiet if that's what you want. Bathcombe's maybe marginally more lively and The Royal Hotel's a good place. Mind you,' she said but hesitated fractionally, 'I'd enjoy feeding you up and as you can see we're not too busy right now. Sorry, I didn't mean to pry. You just enjoy your dinner. I'll leave you to it.'

Before Daisy could reply she left abruptly as though regretting her words.

Daisy had already decided she would stay at The Skittish Pony for a while. She felt it was right for her and she had to learn again to trust her instincts. Now she concentrated on the food. How long since she'd tasted real, home-cooked food? She'd had no appetite these past months and before that the sandwiches and half-finished pizzas snatched in the brief breaks of her hospital day hardly warranted the term real food.

'I've not left a thing,' she murmured guiltily as Martha came to clear the dishes when she had finished.

'There's a girl. A pleasure to feed, you'd be. Only cheese and fruit for dessert, but local cheese and fruit from the garden. Coffee directly.'

'No coffee, thanks. I enjoyed the wine and the meal was wonderful.'

She yawned.

'A stroll outside then early to bed, I think.'

'Get up when you're ready. Breakfast at your convenience.'

Daisy managed a small stab at the cheese and was about to leave the table when three men came into the bar, all three big and burly, all wearing chunky-looking jackets.

'Evening, Bob. Anything planned tonight?'

Bob looked meaningfully towards Daisy who'd sank back into her seat when the men entered. The men looked towards her but didn't speak. Daisy bent her head and fiddled with slivers of cheese, her confidence draining, suddenly aware she was conspicuous here. However, the men ignored her and turned to order their drinks. Huddling close they spoke in low voices, conferring with Bob.

She pushed back her chair on the stone flags as softly as she could and slipped outside. They'd surely be talking about her. Paranoia threatened to take hold but with an effort she pushed it away. It was perfectly normal for men to comment on lone women in a pub, especially in such a rural, moorland spot. It was impossible that anyone here would know anything about her and if they did, why should they care? She gave herself a common-sense sort of shake and remembered her debt to Aunt Lucy.

As she stood uncertainly outside The Skittish Pony a bunch of cyclists swept round the bend and on to the green in front of the inn and were soon dismounting, undoing helmets, stretching, rubbing calves. Several of them nodded to Daisy and one approached her with a list.

'Could we have our drinks out here, a dozen packets of crisps and . . . '

'Sorry, I don't work here. I've just had dinner and . . . '

'Oh, sorry,' the young man said and backed away.

'No problem. Here's the landlord now.'

Bob came out and nodded to Daisy before dealing with the thirsty cyclists.

'Don't go far, Miss Weston, it'll be dark soon and 'tis too easy to get lost even a mile or so from here.'

'No, I'll keep the inn in sight, thanks.'

The road rose steeply above the inn and she followed it, keeping close to a rough stone wall. At the top she looked back. Twilight was softening the scene below her and she could hear the cyclists chattering like rooks at dusk.

Jack and Martha flitted amongst the customers with trays of drinks. A car's headlights cut through the growing dusk, then turned into the carpark.

It was so normal and untroubled it already seemed a thousand light years from London and all that represented. She would stay for a few days, explore the area, maybe move on, maybe stay. She was a free agent, free to make her own choices. That felt good.

Next morning, a tentative knock and Martha's soft, country voice, slightly anxious, startled her from deep sleep.

'Miss Weston, it's well past ten o'clock. Are you all right?'

Daisy sat up. Ten o'clock! She'd slept over twelve hours. A miracle!

'A pot of tea?'

Martha opened the door,

'Please. I'm so sorry, I'd no idea . . . '

'I didn't want to wake you but Bob thought you'd maybe plans for the day. It's the most glorious morning.'

Martha put the tray on the bedside table and pulled back the curtains to let dazzlingly bright golden sunshine into the room.

'I hope I did right to wake you.'

'Of course. I mustn't waste such a wonderful day.'

'Breakfast?'

'Isn't it too late?'

'Gracious, no. We've no set times here, and I do the cooking.'

'Can I . . . I'd like to stay a few days.'

Was it Daisy's imagination or did the faintest shadow of doubt pass over Martha's face? If it was there, it vanished before Daisy could blink and there was no mistaking the warmth in Martha's reply.

'Of course. Just as long as you like. We've a party of walkers booked in next month, and maybe a little passing trade . . . '

'I'd like to explore, it's so beautiful here.'

'You wouldn't think so in winter. We're often cut off for days in severe weather. Then you'd know what isolation is.'

An involuntary shiver ran through Daisy. Mental isolation had been her constant companion these last months and she reckoned she could cope with the physical isolation imposed by a winter on the moor.

'Breakfast in fifteen minutes,' Martha said as she picked up the tray. 'I hope you're hungry.'

'As a horse,' Daisy was amazed to hear herself say.

She couldn't remember when she last had a proper breakfast, even in childhood. Her mother would occasion-ally attempt a Sunday breakfast and, full of good intentions, she would clatter pans, start frying bacon, set on the coffee machine, then would wander away and forget it all leaving her daughter to rescue it as best she could for herself and a tight-lipped, dourly-disapproving father.

Perfectly cooked rashers, grilled tomatoes, mushrooms, golden-yolked fried egg, toast and coffee appeared. Why wasn't this place in the guide books with four stars? She was glad it wasn't otherwise she wouldn't be alone in the dining section of the bar. It was heaven sent, the memory of wraith-like figure in the city bedsit receding more every minute, energy returning to her mind and body.

Daisy persuaded Martha to have coffee with her.

'A great breakfast. I haven't had such food for years.'

'Do you not cook for yourself then?' Martha looked surprised.

'No.'

'But haven't you got someone?'

'Tell me about the village,' Daisy interrupted quickly. 'How many people? What do they do?'

Martha put her cup down carefully.

'Only a few hundred in the actual village, mainly retired folk, farmers trying to make a living. You're not a journalist, are you?'

Suspicion tinged her voice.

'No, of course not. Just interested. I've always lived in London and I'm very ignorant about country life, real country life.'

'Do you never have holidays?'

'Not very often, a few days at the seaside, but my father was always too busy and Mother, well, she was usually doing something else.'

Martha got up.

'Each to his own. City life wouldn't suit me. Now, about supper, I'm going to market this morning. What would you like?'

'Where's that? And please, whatever you cook'll be great.'

'Bathcombe, seven miles on, small but it's got most things. Will you want a packed lunch?'

'Goodness, not after that breakfast. I'd like to walk this morning.'

'You be careful. Easy to . . . '

'I know, to get lost. I'll follow the paths.'

'Bob's got some maps, set walks, talk to him before you go.'

Martha had instinctively warmed to Daisy right away but there was something odd about her. She was guarded, lacked spontaneity, had a sad air of loneliness. She picked up her tray.

'See you later then, Miss Weston.'

'Yes, and it's Daisy, please.'

Martha nearly dropped the tray. Daisy's smile lit up her face and for the first time Martha saw that Daisy Weston was lovely. Her hazel eyes shone with warmth and there was a vitality about her that was quite new.

'I'm glad you'll be staying with us.'

Martha smiled and went to give Bob his orders for the vegetables.

It took Daisy most of the morning to complete Bob's beginner's walk! The path was well marked, over the moor, through a tiny hamlet and back along a rough track which would eventually lead, according to Bob's map, to the other end of the village. She followed a small stream away from the track and it was there she found it, well away from the main track — a tumbledown barn and a couple of more reasonable-looking low, stone buildings, maybe part of a farm farther up the moor?

Leaving the stream, she crossed another track, over a rough patch of ground and there, practically hidden by tall grass and overgrown trees, was a stone cottage. Brambles thrust thorny stems through broken windows. Daisy blinked. She didn't notice the sagging roof, broken guttering and peeling paint but saw a picture-book cottage restored to its former glory set in a well-tended orchard, a flower-filled garden and a red brick path leading to a front door with roses and honeysuckle twining over the porch.

She visualised cool, quiet interiors, polish, pot pourri, bird song — a home, the home she'd never had, the perfect retreat! The **For Sale** sign tacked to the remains of a rotting front gate looked new. She walked all around it, peering in through grimy windows, tempted to look for an entry point, but front and back doors were well secured.

Rummaging in her bag she wrote down the agent's name and practically ran the couple of miles back to The Skittish Pony.

Bob looked up from his paper.

'Miss Weston, what's to do? Martha's not back.'

Daisy shook her head and tried to get her breath back.

'That cottage . . . edge of the moor, by a wood . . . for sale . . . how long?' she gasped out and sat down on a stool by the bar.

In the dim light she hadn't noticed there was someone else there, a man in overalls and a baseball cap. He stared at her then at Bob.

'Does she mean the Jewson place?' he said slowly.

'Reckon so. Elderflower Cottage. Old heap of stones, falling to pieces, three miles back?'

'It must be the one. It's not falling down and it looks very solid, bit of decorating, new windows . . . '

'Bit of decorating! You can't be

serious. The place has been empty 'round about ten years. Pair of spinsters, went a bit dotty.'

'Mabel and Eveline,' the man in the cap added, 'no relatives, intestate. Sale board went up only yesterday.'

'Miss Weston,' Bob said, 'where are you going?'

But Daisy was already gone and the two men heard the car leave in a scrunch of tyres. The man in the bar pushed his empty glass towards Bob.

'You thinking what I am?'

'Maybe,' Bob said as he pulled a pint into the glass. 'Don't seem very likely though, young girl on her own.'

'You don't know that — other half at home perhaps. From London, you say? No end of daft city people prepared to pay a fortune for a heap of rubble, spend another fortune doing it up and then find they don't like rural life. Too quiet, too far from the supermarkets. Always another fool waiting to buy, tear it down, start again.'

'Mmm.'

Bob had heard all this before.

'Won't be popular,' the man went on. 'Folks round here don't like change.'

'Who says there's going to be change?'

The man shrugged and gazed into his pint. Bob took out a wallet and pulled out a business card. He recalled that months ago, a man had come in asking questions about the area, wanting to know about land for sale. He'd been interested in Elderflower Cottage and he'd make it worthwhile if Bob would let him know if it ever came on the market.

'Local knowledge,' the man had said, and pushed some notes over the counter with a wink.

Bob had taken the notes and forgotten all about it until that girl had come and gone like a whirlwind. His hand hovered over the phone, then he put the card back. He hadn't told Martha about the notes. Best leave things. It was some time ago and probably of little significance. Dismissing the problem, he went back to his newspaper.

★   ★   ★

Peter Macey, Bathcombe's only estate agent, had a much more pressing problem, one not to be dismissed so lightly. He stared gloomily at his e-mail message. Tim Burden again, wanting an immediate answer and what was wrong with Macey's phone? Peter had switched to answerphone days ago to avoid making a decision on Tim Burden's offer. Burden's schemes, if implemented, were very likely to interfere with Peter's own business ventures but he couldn't see a solution and time was running out.

'Sonia,' he called unnecessarily loudly as his secretary-cum-receptionist-cum-dogsbody was only a few feet away in the tiny office they shared.

'Yes, still here.'

'Coffee?' he asked hopefully.

'You're behind time. It's lunchtime more likely. Care for a sandwich at The Feathers?'

'Not today, a few things to sort out. You go. I'll look after the office.'

'We're not exactly run off our feet.'

She reached for her jacket.

'Spoke too soon. We have a customer.'

She busily shuffled papers before looking up.

'Can I help you?'

Daisy looked from one to the other.

'I hope so. I've come about Elderflower Cottage.'

'We're about to close,' Sonia said sharply.

Peter stood up.

'Of course we're not. You run along, Sonia, I'll deal with . . . er . . . '

'Daisy Weston. I'd like details of the cottage and, if I could, view inside as soon as possible.'

'You mean as a buyer?' Sonia muttered.

'It is for sale? The board outside . . . '

'Correct.'

Peter came from behind his desk.

'Sonia, you'll be late.'

He hustled her to the door.

'But I needn't . . . '

'Go,' he hissed, opened the door and almost pushed her out before coming back and setting a chair for Daisy opposite his desk. 'A few details first, Miss Weston, then it happens I have an appointment out that way this afternoon. If you're really interested in Elderflower Cottage and its adjoining acres I can take you there right away.'

He pulled out a file, extracted some sheets and handed them over to her.

'Adjoining acres?'

She looked surprised.

'Yes. There's ten acres, a wood, a small paddock, several outbuildings. Did you not see that on the board?'

'No, I didn't, but that's even better.'

A choking excitement gripped Daisy. She hardly dared to think it but a purpose, a plan, was already shaping in her head. Positive thoughts at last.

'Yes, Mr . . . er . . . I'm definitely interested.'

'Peter Macey.'

He held out his hand.

'Pleased to meet you, Miss Weston.'

His grip was firm, his smile friendly. Daisy liked him straight away. She returned the handshake and smiled.

'I'm not in a chain and I have sufficient cash for an immediate purchase.'

Peter Macey could hardly believe what he was hearing but he had to say, 'It does need some work on it. Is it for yourself to live in?'

'It would be, yes.'

Peter hesitated.

'Just you? You don't mind my asking?'

'No, I don't mind,' Daisy said, amused. 'Don't I look like a potential householder?'

'Of course, of course. Sorry, I shouldn't have . . . '

'Don't worry. Shall we go?'

Peter stared at her as though she

might disappear if he took his eyes off her. He couldn't believe his luck. This highly-attractive woman appears out of nowhere with a possible answer to his prayer, or at least a possible postponement of a problem. She was scanning the details he'd given her.

'Only just on the market and a lot of interest already. Sound as a bell structurally, but needs modernising. The two old ladies, born and lived there, not on the cutting edge of technology. I know a good builder, reasonable, and if you like . . . '

'So what are we waiting for?' Daisy said and put the details in her bag.

'Unless you need to have some lunch first.'

'No, no, huge breakfast,' he babbled, grabbing his jacket and taking a set of keys from a cupboard. 'My car's round the back. Just a sec, I need to leave a word for Sonia.'

He scribbled a hasty note and put it on the desk.

'All set,' he said brightly. 'I've a

feeling you're going to love the place.'

'I'm sure I shall,' she replied somewhat dazedly, but still absolutely sure that she was set on the right course.

The note on Sonia's desk read, *If Tim Burden rings or calls I am totally unavailable. On no account mention our new client.*

Sonia read the note when she came back from lunch.

'Well, well,' she mused, tossing it into the waste basket.

The day was turning out to be interesting for a change. She reached for the phone and dialled a familiar number.

3

The broken paving path was choked with weeds and the front door stubbornly refused to open until Peter Macey gave it a hefty, broad-shouldered shove. A stale, musty smell wafted out of the door and, as they stepped inside, something else, too, not particularly pleasant.

'Drains,' Peter said, anxiously watching Daisy. 'Not a problem, just not lived in for years.'

He led the way through the slate-flagged hall to a good-sized room with oak beams and deep window seats.

'It looks as though someone's been living here recently,' Daisy commented, stepping over a heap of dirty blankets cluttered with empty tins and bottles.

'Transient squatters,' Peter said and kicked the blankets. 'I made the place secure last week and arranged for someone to clean up, too. Doesn't look as though they've been yet. Sorry.'

'It doesn't matter.'

Daisy moved to the window. Peter tried to gauge his client's interest. She seemed to have gone off the boil after her initial eagerness.

'Kitchen, pretty basic, through the back,' he said dispiritedly.

'Yes, in a minute. This room could be lovely. It's quite large, south-facing, and once the garden's laid out . . . '

Daisy took a deep breath and ran her hands over the stone embrasures.

'I've always wanted window seats looking out to a real cottage garden.'

Peter perked up.

'So you can see the potential?'

'I'd like to make a phone call.'

She took out her mobile.

'Don't you want to see the rest of the place?'

'In a minute. Could you . . . um . . . ?'

She nodded towards the door.

'Sorry, of course.'

Obediently he went into the hall.

He'd have given a lot to eavesdrop but there was something about Miss Weston which told him that wouldn't do. He moved into the garden, well away from temptation. Inside Daisy waited.

'Please, please be in. Yes, thank goodness. Aunt Lucy, it's me and I've found it.'

'Sorry, I was in the garden. What have you found? Where are you?'

'I'm in Devon, on the moors, and there's this perfect cottage. I'm standing in the living-room now. The sun's pouring in, there's outbuildings, a barn, a wood, a stream, land, about ten acres. I could do so much. You must come down and . . . '

'Whoa, let me get my breath back. Isn't it a bit early? Shouldn't you look around more, and what would you want with all that land and buildings?'

'I've all sorts of plans. I'll need your help, but as soon as I saw it I knew. It's called Elderflower Cottage. Of course there's work to be done and it hasn't been lived in for years . . . '

'What price are they asking and what work has to be done?'

Daisy named the price and made up the building costs. Lucy Weston thought hard and did some fast mental calculations.

'All right, it's within the budget. We'll talk terms later. There's enough in your account for the deposit. I'll transfer the rest as soon as necessary, and make sure you get a proper survey, offer subject to that being OK.'

'Aunt Lucy, you are wonderful. I'm with the agent right now. He says there's a lot of interest in the place.'

'Well, he would, wouldn't he?' Lucy snorted.

'I believe him. It's great property. Wouldn't you like to see it first?'

'No,' was the firm answer. 'Go ahead, your decision, your project. I'll help when needed. Trust your judgement.'

Daisy bit her lip and remembered what bad judgement had already done to her life. Did she have enough confidence to make this major decision on a complete change of life? Was there an alternative? She looked around the neglected room and saw its walls, fresh-painted, floors sanded and polished, furnished — a home and her future.

'I will. I must. Thanks, Aunt Lucy. I'll ring you tonight. Oh, and Auntie, please, don't tell Father yet.'

'If that's what you want.'

'I will tell him, if and when all goes through.'

'You're the boss. Good luck, Daisy.'

'Thanks again.'

Daisy joined Peter Macey outside in the sunshine.

'I'd like to buy it, subject to a survey, of course. I'll give the full asking price in return for a guarantee of completion within a month, and permission from the owners to start work right away if the survey's OK.'

'That shouldn't be a problem, and I'm sure the owner will give consent, subject to the usual legal safeguards.'

The estate agent hoped the wild

thumping of his heart wasn't apparent.

'I'll contact the owner's representative right away.'

'I'll write a deposit cheque now. You can hold it until my offer's accepted. I really would like to move in as soon as possible. Do you know a builder who could make it habitable quickly?'

'Oh, yes.'

Peter had an extensive network of useful contacts and it suited his book to have the deal completed without delay before more developers like Burden could make a move.

'I'll get back to the office and start things moving now.'

'I thought you had another appointment in the area.'

'That'll keep,' he said airily.

'I'd like to see over the rest of the property, walk the land, look in the outbuildings. I see they're padlocked. You have the keys?'

'Er . . . no. Those outbuildings are rented out, storage, local farmer, I believe.'

'Don't you know?' Daisy frowned. 'I shall need them for my own use. Could you check the leases, see when they can be vacated?'

'Sure.'

Peter hadn't expected this, but no matter, he'd at least got a temporary reprieve, a breathing space. He was very much a believer in the sufficient-unto-the-day philosophy. Now he couldn't wait to telephone Tim Burden to tell him the Elderflower property was off the market. Surreptitiously he looked at his watch.

'It may take a while to walk the entire estate, and I really should make those calls, contact the owners.'

He fingered the cheque Daisy had just written.

'All right, we'll just do the cottage and you show me the boundaries.'

'Sure. I'll leave you a map. The boundaries are drawn in red.'

'That'll do, and perhaps if you've any news you'll contact me tonight at The Skittish Pony. I'll give you my

48

mobile number.'

'Very wise. The village grapevine is rampant.'

Daisy was relieved to see the bar was deserted when she got back. She went to her room, had a leisurely bath and only went downstairs when Polly, Martha's helper, knocked to say supper was on the table. Martha, naturally, knew all about Daisy's interest in Elderflower Cottage.

'Well, now,' she said, putting a basket of home-made bread on the table, 'Bob tells me you were enquiring about Elderflower Cottage. Not serious surely?'

'Oh, no,' Daisy lied, 'just for comparison with London prices. I passed it on my walk that's all. Wonderful soup, Martha.'

Martha sensed the evasion and wisely held her tongue.

Daisy hated to lie to Martha but the dream was too fragile to share as yet. She needed to keep it in her own head. After dinner she worked on her lap-top in her room until late. Just after dinner, Peter Macey had phoned.

'Great news. The owner accepts your offer and is just as eager to complete as you are.'

'Really? That was quick. Is it truly going ahead? I can't believe it.'

'No second thoughts?'

'Not in the slightest.'

'Good, because I've lined up a builder pal of mine and he'll see us at the property early in the morning.'

'You're a genius.'

Peter was on a high after telling Tim Burden Elderflower Cottage and land were no longer for sale. Burden had blustered and threatened, then increased his offer by twenty per cent. Peter was duty bound to pass on the offer but reckoned he was safe. He knew something about the vendors Tim Burden didn't and wouldn't understand in a million years if he did.

The summer sun was already clearing the dawn mists when Daisy woke next morning. For a while she lay and thought about the cottage, excitement and hope running in equal measure. No sounds from below. It was too early for breakfast. She'd visit her property! Dressing quickly she went softly down the stairs.

' 'Morning, Miss Weston.'

Bob, at his usual post behind the bar with newspaper, made her jump guiltily.

'Early bird. Hope the bit of noise here last night didn't disturb you.'

'I didn't hear anything. Slept like a log but it's so lovely I thought a stroll before breakfast. You're early, too.'

He came round the bar and shot back the bolts.

'I don't sleep much. Take care. I'll tell Martha. Going far?'

'No. Thanks.'

She slipped out and waited. Bob stood at the doorway watching. She gave a wave. He waved back but didn't go in.

'Oh, well.'

She shrugged. Nothing unusual about going for a stroll by car. She gave

Bob another wave as the car shot off towards Elderflower Cottage.

It sat in the warm sun, already comfortingly familiar. She patted the wall possessively.

'Just wait, soon you won't recognise yourself.'

She turned away. It was the wood that Peter Macey had indicated with a vague hand sweep which drew her. Pretty, he'd said, quite small, local picnic spot, couples, that sort of thing. She hadn't cared much for that. Part of the attraction of the place was its isolation. Maybe she'd get a dog. She'd always wanted one but her father had always condemned the idea.

Before entering what she thought of as her wood she turned back to get the perspective on her cottage. The sun glinted on the cracked window panes with an approving wink and she winked back before walking into the cool green depths of Bluebell Wood.

Only a few yards in, yet the enchantment of the place caught and held her still to listen to the morning bird song and to watch sunlight pattern the leafy floor. A well-trodden path led her towards the heart as she breathed in the dense woodland smell of summer. It was a long time, if ever, that she'd felt such peace and harmony with her surroundings. The sensation was calming and Daisy instinctively knew this wood would always work its magic for her. She closed her eyes holding the moment, praying it really would be hers, and soon!

The spell broke as a flock of birds rose from the trees, flapping skywards in twittering panic. A dog barked, Daisy jumped, caught her foot in a tree root, falling to her knees. There was a sharp snap of steel, more barking, and a man's voice called out urgently. A huge black dog came crashing through the bushes, checked momentarily when it saw Daisy on the ground, then lunged towards her, teeth bared. She screamed, tried to get up, but her foot was caught fast.

'Leo, down, down.'

The command halted the animal at once. The dog sank to the ground, ears twitching, brown eyes fastened on Daisy.

'Get away,' she yelled. 'Shoo, you great brute.'

Feeling along the ground she picked up a small log and threw it at the dog. It grazed its nose as it rose slightly, a threatening sort of whirr grumbling in its throat. She picked up another log.

'Don't be such a fool. Keep still. Here, boy. Leo, heel.'

Instantly the dog got up, backed away, then trotted towards the man now standing only a few feet away from Daisy, tall, broad-shouldered, brown-haired, with dark eyes flashing furious anger at Daisy.

'What are you doing here? Good heavens!' His voice was even angrier. 'Don't you see how near you are to that trap? An inch or two closer and your leg would've been snapped in half.'

'Traps! I don't believe it.'

She tugged furiously at the root.

'What is this, the Dark Ages? Are you responsible for that contraption?'

With a final jerk she freed her foot and scrambled to her feet.

'Don't move and keep still. There may be another one close by. Stay exactly where you are. Leo, keep close.'

Daisy shook with fury.

'How can you be so stupid as to plant those things where people walk?'

'People have no business in here. It's private property. There are plenty of notices.'

As he spoke he trod around the undergrowth, prodding it with a stick.

'Notices which say **Trespassers will be prosecuted**, or are you one of those townie tourists who thinks they know the countryside better than those of us who live here? Come down for a few days' holiday, ignore the rules and lay down the law about how we should behave on our own land.'

'How dare you talk to . . . '

He came closer and interrupted her sharply.

'I've seen you somewhere before, the other evening, skulking on the moor,' he snapped. 'You're not an animal rights protester or a journalist?'

'No, I'm not, and you've no call to be so insufferably pompous. And I was not skulking. I was walking.'

'Trespassing.'

'The moor is private property, is it?'

'Some of it, and you're trespassing in here, for sure.'

'You don't own this wood, unless of course you're a relative of the late Misses Pewson.'

'What?'

Daisy was delighted at what Aunt Lucy would have described as having the air knocked out from under his ribs.

'The Pewsons? Elderflower Cottage? Ah!'

Daisy saw that his eyes were deep hazel.

'So, it's true. I didn't connect. Stupid of me. I should have guessed.'

He was interrupted by a loud, 'Halloo there, Miss Weston?' and Peter Macey appeared.

The dog rose, the low growling rumbling from his throat instantly stilled by a gesture from the man.

'Macey,' he said, 'I might have guessed. This,' he indicated Daisy who was brushing leaves from her clothes, 'must be the interested client.'

Peter looked annoyed.

'How did you . . . ? Ah, don't tell me. Your friend, Sonia. Not much of a personal assistant, blabbing out office secrets at the first opportunity.'

'Not necessarily Sonia. You know how news travels round here.'

He turned to Daisy, his dark eyes assessing her anew.

'You must be Daisy Weston, staying at The Skittish Pony and interested in Elderflower Cottage.'

'I . . . '

But having thus pigeon-holed her he turned back to Peter Macey.

'Of course you can't do that. You

know we're interested in the land.'

'You didn't make an offer,' Peter Macey snapped.

'We've been too busy,' the stranger exploded. 'My grandfather approached the old ladies . . . '

'Years ago, before my time. Why should I come cap-in-hand to you? I'm not in your feudal manor, and Miss Weston's offer has already been accepted. I've set the ball rolling and we have permission to start work on the cottage right away.'

'You can't do that,' the man repeated. 'You're duty bound to accept the best offer. We'll top anything she's offered.'

Daisy's anger, simmering ever since the stranger had appeared, finally boiled.

'Don't be so rude. After the way you've behaved this morning I'm totally determined to have Elderflower Cottage. I won't be bullied out of it by anyone.'

'Good for you, Miss Weston,' Macey

applauded. 'This is Jack Hawksworth. His family has farmed here for centuries and they believe that gives them the right to do exactly as they please. They used to be a power in the neighbourhood but not now. I hear farming's not doing too well these days, Hawksworth.'

'That's none of your business,' the man said grimly, 'and I insist you pass over our offer to whoever owns the place.'

'Not possible, I'm afraid. It's too late. I have rather unusual instructions from my clients. I was to accept the first full asking price and honour it at all costs, no deals, auctions or gazumping. You see, the Misses Pewsons' long-lost relatives, when finally traced, turn out to be rare birds, Ian and Milly Pewson, the old girls' nephew and niece. They are Christian missionaries working in remote areas of Africa. They're not interested in money. They were very specific, the first cash buyer, and that person is Miss Weston. Her cheque is already in the bank. I deposited it last night.'

A dark scowl clouded Jack Hawksworth's face and his voice was grim.

'In spite of what you say I insist you put in a further, higher offer to the vendors and I shall require evidence you've done so, and of the vendors' response. I don't believe or trust you. We've every right to that land. There's more to this and I intend to find out what.'

'Excuse me,' Daisy spoke crisply, 'I don't want to be drawn into this argument. My business is with Mr Macey here and as for you, Mr Hawksworth, you owe me an apology for being so offensively rude, and for setting your dog on me.'

She stood tall, her green eyes fixed on Jack Hawksworth. He blinked as though seeing her for the first time.

'Apology? I don't see why, and as for setting Leo on you, that is ridiculous. He's as docile as a kitten. I believed you were trespassing.'

'It's not your land. It's you who are trespassing.'

Daisy stood her ground. Jack now looked bemused.

'He'll never see that,' Peter said. 'The Hawksworths believe they have rights over the whole local community.'

'Not over me they don't,' she said, turning to Jack. 'Your disagreement with Mr Macey is nothing to do with me. I'll see you back at the cottage, Mr Macey. Don't be too long. I don't want to be late for breakfast.'

Rather than feeling intimidated, she was exhilarated by the confrontation. She relished the challenge and was delighted to find her old spirit reasserting itself — a sure sign she was on the road to recovery.

4

Martha looked with approval at Daisy's clean plate, and said happily, 'You're a joy to feed and you're looking a lot better than when you first arrived here.'

'It's your great cooking, Martha. I'm sure I've put on a few pounds. I expect you've heard we may be neighbours soon.'

No point in keeping it secret now and she rightly suspected Martha knew already.

'So I believe. Not just a price comparison to London then?'

'No. Sorry about that deception but it was too early to be sure and even now there could be setbacks.'

She poured Martha a cup of coffee.

'It's the oddest thing,' Martha said as she sat down opposite Daisy. 'Elderflower Cottage has been empty for years and now suddenly it's what they term a hot property. Everyone's after it, it seems.'

'Everyone?'

Anxiety clutched at Daisy's heart.

'The Hawksworths have always wanted to gobble up the land. It's adjacent to theirs. Old Jacob Hawksworth, now long dead, Mr Jack's grandfather, thought he had a natural right to it, just assumed, so the story goes, that the old girls would automatically leave it to the Hawksworths. He was very friendly with both the Pewson girls and rumour has it . . . well, never mind . . . let's just say he was a pretty regular visitor to the cottage.'

Daisy was wide-eyed, suddenly seeing her cottage in a more romantic, albeit sinister, light.

'Then Bob told me only this morning of a gentleman regularly nosing round the area looking for land. He asked Bob to be sure to tell him if the empty cottage and land ever came on the market. 'Course, Bob forgot all about it until you turned up. Probably a property developer.'

'So there are serious would-be buyers out there.'

'Seems so. I can't say I relish building development here. It'd ruin the village and the Hawksworths are a mite too cocky for my liking although perhaps not so much now as in the past. Farming's hard and they're doing their best to do other things to survive. Would it be just you living there?'

Martha was tentative, didn't want to pry, but she was worried about Daisy who seemed vulnerable and no match for all the sharks around.

'Yes. Just me and maybe a dog for company.'

'Well, it's pretty enough in the summer but in winter, it's very isolated. What would you do there?'

'I've got plans but I'd rather not . . . '

'Naturally, but wouldn't you be lonely after London life?'

'I hate London,' Daisy said vehemently. 'I can't live there any more and I need a fresh start.'

'Well, I'd love to have you here as a neighbour even though the cottage is three or four miles away but do think hard, Daisy. Country life is very different from town. Folk can be hard to get to know. They don't like change and I have to say they can be a bit wary of newcomers.'

'You're not a bit like that.'

Martha laughed.

'I'll tell you something. I'm an outsider, too, born in Bathcombe. Bob's the local. The Skittish Pony's been in his family for generations so I'm tolerated.'

She stood up.

'If you do decide Elderflower Cottage is what you want just keep a low profile to begin with, and any help you need, Bob and I'll be glad to give.'

She put a motherly arm round Daisy's shoulders.

'And we'll wish you good luck, too.'

'Thanks, Martha. I'll need it, I'm sure, but it really is what I want. Truly.'

'Then you'll be fine because that's half the battle.'

'May I stay on here a few days more, keep an eye on things?'

' 'Course you can. The place is livelier with you here. Stay as long as you want — special discount for locals!' she teased.

Peter Macey had a genius for pushing things along and within a week his builder friend plus mates had the cottage more or less habitable although Daisy couldn't actually move in until contracts were exchanged. Instead, she worked on the garden, supervised by a guy Peter knew who was a first class gardener.

'Maybe you'll be in by a week or two,' the estate agent promised Daisy. 'I have a solicitor acting for you and the vendor. That speeds things up and he knows how to cut a few corners.'

'Oh, no, don't do anything to jeopardise the sale.'

'Don't worry. It's as safe as houses. Nothing can go wrong, I promise.'

There was no point in telling Daisy about Tim Burden's increasingly abusive threats to his own person, or the continuing pressure from the Hawksworths to persuade the owners to take a better offer. Fortunately he had broad shoulders and the relatives in Africa, to his amazement, stood by their principles and refused all other offers. It was time for Daisy to tell her parents her plans. Her heart sank when her father answered the call.

'Daisy, where are you?'

Sharp annoyance fairly rattled down the phone line. As quickly as she could she explained her plan, and held her breath. There was an ominous silence before the explosion.

'Absolute nonsense. I've never heard such a hair-brained notion. Lucy had no right to interfere.'

'She didn't!'

'I'll be the judge of that,' he said grimly. 'I'll speak to her later. You are to come home at once. I've got a job for you, locum in the private sector, a group of hospitals. The director's a friend of mine who's prepared to overlook that other business! It's the best chance you'll get.'

Daisy felt faint and her voice refused to function.

'Daisy, you there? Answer me, please.'

She made a tremendous effort.

'Yes . . . and . . . um . . . I'm not going to argue and I'm grateful for your offer but I've already made my decision. I'm staying here. I couldn't possibly take that job. I'm through with hospitals. Please give my love to Mother and don't worry about me. I'll phone again.'

She immediately put down the phone. She didn't yet have the confidence for a major confrontation with her father, indeed had she ever? Was there ever a time she'd stood up to him? She doubted it but at long last she knew she had to go her own way in life and make her own decisions.

For the next few days she worked

hard clearing ground and listening to the advice of Peter's gardening friend. Then after supper back at the inn she worked on her lap-top scouring the internet and building up an impressive data base on her project.

A party of walkers was booked in to The Skittish Pony for a week so Martha and Bob were well occupied and Daisy's time was her own. She was happy and the days flew by.

One day Peter Macey found her as usual working in the garden with the building gang hammering and sawing in the background.

'Completion date a week today,' he announced.

Daisy dropped her fork and flung her arms round him.

'You genius! At last, though I do know it's the speediest ever, but if you only knew how I long to be in there and call Elderflower Cottage mine!'

'Wow, that's the first time a client's done that,' Peter said hoarsely, shaken by Daisy's body contact.

'Sorry,' she said and moved away quickly, 'but you've helped me such a lot. I truly am grateful. I'd never have got it without you.'

You most certainly wouldn't, Peter thought grimly, not a chance, but it had worked in his interest as well. He looked at his client, flushed with pleasure, the smudge of earth on her cheek adding to the attraction. Her chestnut hair was longer, thicker. She'd changed since that first day she'd come into his office. He'd been attracted then.

'So, may I take you out to dinner to celebrate?' he asked.

'Oh, I don't think . . . there's no need.'

'I'd like to.'

'I'm going away for a while.'

'Away? Now?'

'Only a few days. I'll be back for completion day, of course.'

'When you come back then?' he persisted.

'We'll see. I'll be busy moving in.'

70

'I'll help. I know a guy . . . '

'I'm sure you do,' Daisy said, laughing. 'It's a deal, after moving day.'

No harm in supper. She liked Peter, felt comfortable with him, and he had been very helpful. It'd be good to have a little social life again. She found she looked forward to it.

In fact, she was reluctant to leave the village at all although she'd only shuttled between The Skittish Pony and Elderflower Cottage so far. It was time to take the next step, before she went to see Aunt Lucy.

The village street was deserted. The small post office and general store looked shuttered and closed even though a crooked notice said it was open. Feeling oddly nervous, Daisy pushed open the door, and nearly shot out again. It was crowded. There was a queue at the post office counter and a cluster of customers around the self-service section in the main store.

The noisy hum of conversation and laughter ceased abruptly the moment

71

Daisy walked in. Everyone looked at her, but no-one said a word. She stood rooted to the spot wishing herself anywhere but where she was. The familiar paranoia took hold and as the conversational buzz broke out again she felt everyone was talking about her.

She sidled to the back of the post office counter shrinking into herself, praying for invisibility. Perhaps she could slip out unnoticed, but the doorbell jangled and a tall figure filled the doorway.

'Afternoon.'

His smile embraced everyone, checking in surprise at Daisy. All the women smiled back, calling out greetings.

'Now, Jack,' the large motherly figure behind the till spoke out. 'How's things? Busy?'

'We are now. Full tilt, no vacancies, thank goodness. Ma sent me to pick up a load of stuff for the freezer.'

'Yes, she phoned earlier. I'll get it, it's all ready. Shan't be long,' she said to the waiting customers who appeared to accept the queue-jumping as perfectly natural.

The atmosphere became more animated, everyone joining in the chat. Daisy, watching from the sidelines, wouldn't have been the least surprised to find someone bustling about with tea and biscuits all round. She was grateful for the diversion which preserved her anonymity.

'Have any of you met Miss Weston yet?'

Jack's voice carried through the shop, snapping Daisy right into the limelight.

'She's the latest newcomer to the community. She's bought Elderflower Cottage. It'll be good to see it lived in again.'

Now Daisy was truly the focus of attention and everyone had an excuse to stare openly, but the faces were friendlier, curious but with no hostility. Several murmured a greeting. Daisy tried her best to smile at everyone, at the same time remembering the stamps she'd come in for. She made her purchase, exchanged more nods and smiles and left quickly.

Outside, she leaned against the wall, heart hammering. For a brief instance in that village store the austere London courtroom scene had flashed before her, all those faces, hostile, condemning, sad anger in the faces of the child's parents, the consultant, Guy Peterson, his face averted, never meeting her eyes. She waited for the image to fade, for strength to return to her jellied legs, strength enough to walk away.

'Hi, Miss Weston, are you all right? What's wrong?'

It was Jack Hawksworth, all six foot three of him, watching her with concern.

'Nothing. Leave me alone, please.'

'You look terrible. What sent you scuttling out of the post office so fast?'

Indignation was a good treatment for panic.

'I didn't scuttle. It was a bit startling with everyone looking at me.'

'Oh, that. I was just being friendly. If

you're going to live here you should get to know people. It's what you do in the country otherwise, unless you're going to be popping back to the city every five minutes, you're going to find it lonely. Elderflower Cottage isn't just another second country home, is it?'

His disapproval was tangible.

'What if it is? It's none of your business.'

'It is though. It's my village, my community. It's best for it if people live and work here all the time. Fortunately the grapevine tells me you are going to be a permanent resident so that's OK.'

'Magnanimous of you.'

Daisy moved away from the wall but he blocked her way.

'Look, let's start again. I didn't follow you out of the shop to argue. I followed you because I wanted to apologise for the other morning, in the wood. It was unpardonable. My only excuse is there's a lot going on at High Ridge, our farm and holiday business. I wasn't thinking straight. I'm sorry. I hope you'll forgive me and we can be friends, or good neighbours at least.'

Daisy eyed him with deep suspicion. She didn't trust him. He was being too charming, too amenable. She remembered his frustrated anger over Elderflower Cottage that morning in the wood.

'You've every right to buy the cottage,' he went on. 'We've been unbusinesslike, assuming we could snap it up any time. We've been so busy we never got round to it. Our loss, your gain.'

He held out his hand and smiled. Daisy saw it was a very attractive smile with not the least trace of the other morning's dark fury.

She said, 'That trap, how could I be friends with anyone who does that?'

He dropped his hand and the smile vanished.

'Steel traps are illegal, and even if they weren't I would never use one. I'm a farmer, not a barbarian.'

'Who then?'

For a moment he didn't reply, simply looked at her, then the post office bell pinged and two women came out.

'Still here, Jack, and er ... Miss Watson?'

'So we are, and it's Weston, Daisy Weston,' Jack answered pleasantly and when the two women were gone said, 'Look, why don't you come and meet my family? See for yourself we're not the arrogant landowners Macey would have you believe, and as we're going to be close neighbours ... '

Daisy tried to get a grip on this new Jack Hawksworth who appeared to have relinquished his desire for her land and cottage so easily. What was he up to? But hadn't Peter assured her nothing could go wrong now? What could the Hawksworths do so near the exchange of contracts?

'That would be very nice,' she said politely, thinking it would be a good move to take a peek into the enemy camp, for that's how she still saw Jack

Hawksworth in spite of his changed persona.

'Great.'

He took her arm.

'My Land-Rover's parked over by the square.'

'I didn't mean now. Later, when I get back.'

'You're going away?'

'Tomorrow, to visit my aunt up North.'

'Well, then, let's make the most of today.'

He guided her across the street, opened the door of his Land-Rover, helped her into the passenger seat, ignoring her protests, and drove off.

Briefly Daisy thought of leaping out but once through the village street Jack turned off into a narrow lane where there was barely room for one vehicle let alone a dramatic escape attempt where she'd probably fall under the wheels. Besides, in a perverse sort of way, she was quite enjoying the sensation of being kidnapped! She stole a glance at his strong profile, such an attractive man who maybe wasn't the monster she'd first thought.

The panic attack outside the shop had completely gone and besides, to a city girl like Daisy, these rural experiences were beginning to take on an interesting novelty although she'd no idea what to expect at the farm.

'We'll take the cross-country route,' Jack said. 'It'll take you near to the cottage and you'll see how close you are to the High Ridge boundary.'

5

Jack stopped the Land-Rover at the top of a high ridge which overlooked moorland sweeping away in rising and falling folds to the distant blue horizon and Daisy caught her breath. So used to rows of streets blotting out the horizon, the open grandeur of the moor overwhelmed her.

'Fantastic,' was too tame a word to describe it. 'Amazing,' she added for good measure.

Jack nodded, satisfied with the reaction. Gently he turned her head and she felt his hand on her hair.

'See, there's Elderflower Cottage behind your land and kingdom, Miss Weston. I hope you'll be happy in your possession of it.'

Daisy listened for bitterness or irony and found none, simply Jack's love of the entire landscape.

'It looks so tiny, like a dolls' house.'

'A valuable property nonetheless. You can just about make out its entire boundaries from here, the wood on one side, the stream on the other. Our land runs from this ridge down to the stream, our shared boundary. The farm's over the other side behind the ridge, hence the name, High Ridge.'

He switched on the ignition then pointed across the fields.

'Those white woolly blobs are Hawksworth sheep. Next we'll see the Hawksworth humans. They aren't quite so docile.'

Daisy had enjoyed the wonderfully exhilarating scenic drive so much she'd forgotten its purpose! High Ridge Farm was the enemy camp! As Jack drove through an open gate marked, **High Ridge Farm and Holiday Complex**, into a cobbled yard, her stomach nerves fluttered.

A good-looking girl leading a horse across the yard turned at the sound of the Land-Rover. Her scowl did little to calm Daisy's unease.

'Where on earth have you been, Jack? Ma's cooking for ten tonight and she's waiting for those things from the village.'

The girl bore a striking resemblance to Jack, and Daisy was reminded of her very first Hawksworth encounter in Bluebell Wood. A volatile family, for this girl was obviously related to Jack. She wondered how many more Hawksworths lived in the stone farmhouse set back from the yard.

'Hold on, Helena,' Jack said mildly, 'no need to be snappy. We have a visitor, and I thought you were taking a riding group this afternoon.'

'I was, but Lightning went lame on me. I may have to call in the vet.'

The scowl darkened as she looked at Daisy.

'You're not a guest, are you? We're terribly busy right now.'

Her tone firmly implied casual visitors of Daisy's ilk were a thorough nuisance to be got rid of without delay or ceremony.

She turned away just as Jack said, 'This is Daisy Weston, soon to live in Elderflower Cottage. Our new neighbour.'

He jumped out of the Land-Rover and came round to open Daisy's door.

'My sister, Helena,' he introduced, 'and evidently not in the best of moods today.'

Helena spun round, her fury blacker than ever.

'So you're the person who's snatched my heritage from under our noses. How you managed it we'll never know. Some devious treachery of Macey's, no doubt, though what he has to gain . . . '

'Stop right there.' Jack's voice cut across hers like a whiplash. 'We've been through this. The family agreed we make the best of it, and you're being incredibly rude. Daisy is not involved in this.'

'So why bring her here?'

Helena thrust out a petulant lip and

Daisy sensed Jack's anger rising as brother and sister glared at each other. She made no move to get down from the passenger seat.

'Nor do I wish to be involved in your argument,' she said sharply. 'I shall be perfectly happy for you to drive me back to village right now, Jack.'

'That's ridiculous,' Jack growled. 'I invited you here and I want you to stay in spite of my sister's behaviour, for which I apologise.'

His withering look of contempt made Helena blink.

'All right, I'm sorry. I've had a bad morning. I think Lightning may need some treatment and I've classes scheduled this evening. You're welcome to High Ridge, Daisy.'

The apology was grudging and Daisy doubted its sincerity but nodded her acknowledgement as Helena turned and walked her lame horse towards the stable block. Jack rolled his eyes heavenwards.

'Sorry about that. My sister can be,

well, a little abrasive at times.'

He hesitated, looked at Daisy as if about to expand then said abruptly, 'She has her reasons, but it was inexcusable. Come into the house, meet my mother.'

'How many more of you?'

Jack laughed.

'Only Ma at the moment. Tim and Molly, the twins, are at college but they'll be home next week. So you're spared the full complement for now.'

'Just your mother?'

'Yes, she's widowed. My father died two years ago.'

'I'm sorry.'

Daisy noted the brief flash of pain in his eyes, intense but quickly controlled. He hauled out the sack of groceries from the Land-Rover and Daisy followed him across the yard to the house. It was built many decades ago, she guessed, from the same local stone as The Skittish Pony. It had small windows and a low door.

'This is the back. The holiday

cottages are the other side. We're building up a regular holiday complex, swimming pool, tennis, riding, providing working holidays for those who fancy a taste of farm life, complete riding weeks. You name it, we'll try it.'

'No real farming then?'

'Oh, yes, that as well but at present we couldn't survive on just the farm. It's diversify or go under!'

He pushed open the door with his shoulder.

'Please go in. Ma's bound to be in the kitchen. Mind your head.'

He stooped and followed her into a slate-flagged passageway. It was quite dark and as Daisy's eyes adjusted, a woman came out to meet them. Wonderful baking smells filled the small hallway. The woman called out.

'Jack, dear, I'm glad you're back. Number Four cottage had a blocked sink. Why, who's this? A visitor?'

'Yes and no. Not a holidaymaker though, more a permanent feature. Daisy Weston, Elderflower Cottage.'

The woman peered briefly at Daisy then opened the kitchen door wide.

'Goodness, do come in where I can see you. I've just put the kettle on and the scones are right out of the oven. Come in, come in.'

A marked contrast to Helena Hawksworth, Marjorie Hawksworth welcomed Daisy enthusiastically. She was tall, upright, a handsome woman exuding a motherly warmth which embraced Daisy immediately, softening the acerbity of the younger Hawksworth. Steaming cups of tea, fragrant scones, home-made jam and thick, Devonshire cream appeared instantaneously. The sack of groceries was dealt with swiftly, then Marjorie Hawksworth sat down to survey her visitor more thoroughly.

'I'm pleased to meet you, Daisy. We've all been wondering about you and what you'll be doing at Elderflower Cottage. No, no, we're not prying but, well, in a rural community likes ours, you can't help being aware. You're much younger than I imagined, don't you think so, too, Jack? Oh, don't forget the blocked sink. They're out for the day so you've a bit of time, and the swimming pool man wants a word.'

'You're evidently very busy,' Daisy said, glancing at her watch. 'I mustn't hold you up. I didn't intend to come at all but . . . '

'I kidnapped her.' Jack smiled. 'I had to show her we intend to become good neighbours.'

'Of course. I hope we see lots more of you, Daisy, particularly when the season's over. It's so busy just now which is very gratifying but with Tim and Donna home, that'll be four extra hands.'

'Do you cook for the holidaymakers, too?' Daisy asked, eyeing the vast quantity of fruit and vegetables on the long pine table.

'On request. There's a family birthday party tonight. I love to do it but it's just there's so much else.'

Daisy stood up.

'And I must go. I'm away for a few

days and there's masses to do at the cottage. I'll be delighted to see you at Elderflower Cottage and I hope . . . '

Mentally, she excluded Helena who at that precise moment chose to burst into the room.

'Mother, is there any tea? We're parched . . . Oh!' She stopped abruptly. 'You're still here.'

'Just going. Thank you, Mrs Hawksworth, for making me so welcome,' Daisy said pointedly as a second person followed Helena into the room and made straight for Jack.

Putting her arms round his neck, she kissed him on the lips, totally ignoring Daisy. Jack swiftly disengaged himself, moving towards the door.

'Hi, Sonia. You have a riding lesson this afternoon? I'm just taking Daisy back to the village. Maybe see you later?'

'I'll be here. Aren't you moving in next week?'

Her words to Daisy were grudging, her eyes fixed all the while on Jack.

'I hope so.'

'And what do you intend doing there?' Sonia asked.

'I'll think of something,' Daisy said evasively. 'Jack, I really must go. I'm sorry to drag you away but I honestly haven't the time to walk back.'

'I wouldn't hear of it, but I'll give you a quick tour of the complex before we go. Back soon. Don't worry, Mum.'

'I'm not. Do come again soon, Daisy.'

'Just what did you do before you came here, Daisy,' Helena drawled, 'before you landed Elderflower Cottage?'

At the door, Daisy turned, aware they were all watching, the two younger women with barely concealed hostility. She felt the familiar flush starting at the neck and she put up a hand to conceal her face.

'I . . . er . . . er . . . worked in London,' she blurted out.

'Yes, but at what?' Helena persisted.

'Don't be so nosey,' Jack said as he

took Daisy's arm. 'Best thing to do is post up your life's history on the village notice board. Just make up what you like then everyone'll be satisfied and leave you alone.'

Sonia had the last word.

'Don't forget, Jack,' she called after them, 'later tonight, remember?'

Jack didn't reply as they walked back across the yard.

'Perhaps we'd best leave the tour of the complex for another time,' he said as he opened the passenger door of the Land-Rover. 'We're all a bit pushed for time right now.'

'Suits me.'

Daisy longed to escape after the intrusive pressure of Helena's and Sonia's questioning. Jack sensed her unease.

'Don't take any notice of those two. Helena will come round.'

He swung the vehicle back across the fields.

'Isn't The Skittish Pony in the other direction, on the main road surely?'

'If it's OK with you I'd like to drop by Elderflower Cottage first. I know a short cut and I'm curious to see how the renovations are progressing.'

Daisy thought for a moment. She hadn't decided about the Hawksworths. Mother seemed lovely, Helena was horrible, and Jack? Jack was Jack and her feeling was ambivalent. She remembered Sonia's proprietorial kiss. Were she and Jack an item?

'OK,' she said, 'but only for a minute.'

When they arrived at the cottage, she felt a familiar rush of pride as they peered in the renewed and now sparkling clean windows.

'The living-room's great, kitchen pretty basic and there's still a mountain of work to be done both inside and out,' she explained.

'Looks fine to me, and once your furniture's in . . . '

'I don't have much.'

She actually didn't own a thing, not even a coffee pot.

'Minimalist. I like that. Too much clutter at High Ridge.'

Jack had left the cottage and was striding around the garden.

'You've put in a lot of work here.'

'Joe Mitchell's been a great help.'

'Joe? Joe's been here?'

'I couldn't have managed without his strength and horticultural wisdom.'

'Horticulture? This huge plot ready for planting? Is this serious gardening? Not just self-sufficiency, is it, for a living?'

He looked sceptical.

'A smallholding? I could give you a list of failed smallholders if you . . . '

'Oh, do mind your own business,' Daisy cried out. 'I've never met so many people interested in my future, so many nosey-parkers who think they can tell me what to do just because I lived in a city and you've all lived in the country since . . . since the Romans conquered Britain. It's . . . it's . . . '

'Arrogant? Unnerving?' Jack said with more than a hint of amused mockery in his eyes. 'I'm afraid you'll have to get used to that if you intend settling here. Tell me, Daisy, in your previous life, which you seem at such pains to conceal, and, no, I don't want to know about it, but wasn't anybody interested in anybody else? Weren't people concerned for each other?'

He put his hands on her shoulders and turned her towards him. His grip tightened, his eyes forcing a response and for a split second she imagined the relief of throwing herself into his arms and pouring out all the hurt and poison she'd suffered in the last months of that previous life.

'Daisy,' he said softly, sensing her uncertainty, bending his head to hers.

Confused, she blurted out, 'I can walk back to The Skittish Pony.'

'Nonsense,' Jack said. 'It's only a couple of minutes' drive.'

They walked over to where the Land-Rover was parked by the locked outbuilding.

'Good storage space in there,' he

94

remarked as he started the engine.

'It will be. It's let out to a farmer.'

'Oh? Who?'

He sounded surprised.

'I don't know. Peter's dealing with it. I'll need it eventually but there's loads of room in the old barn for now.'

Jack hesitated to ask room for what, because he knew by now he wouldn't get an answer. He could only hope time and patience would unlock the secrets of his intriguing new neighbour.

'And you trust Macey?' was all he said.

'Yes, I do. He's been great.'

Tension strung tautly between them once more. Martha's welcome at the inn only slightly diffused it. She was wiping down the garden table when they arrived at The Skittish Pony.

'Why, Jack,' she said as she looked up in surprise, 'how lovely to see you. It's been ages, but I hear you're very busy, so that's good.'

'It is, but Daisy's going away tomorrow so I persuaded her to meet some of the High Ridge Hawksworths.'

'That was nice.'

'So-so. Helena wasn't in the sweetest of tempers.'

'Ah, well. Have you time for a drink?'

'Thanks, but another time. Mother's doing a cooking marathon and, well, you know how it is.'

'I do indeed, which reminds me, Daisy. Those dates you gave were fine except for the night before you move into Elderflower Cottage. We've a long-standing party, a cycle club, an annual event. We're full then but I can get you a room in the village and you can leave your things here.'

'No need,' Jack interrupted. 'Lots of spare rooms at High Ridge.'

'Please, don't worry. I'd already decided. I've got a tent and I'm camping at Elderflower Cottage the night before I move in. I'm looking forward to it.'

'I don't think that's a good idea,' Martha said, frowning.

'Nor do I,' Jack added. 'We'd be

pleased to have you.'

'It's good of you both but I would prefer to stick to my original plan. Now, I really have to pack for tomorrow.'

Jumping down from the Land-Rover, she gave Jack a wave and went into the inn, now so familiar that it felt like home. She was amazed to find she was loathe to leave the village in spite of all its nosey concern.

6

The motorway was busy with late, seasonal traffic. Camper vans and caravans all travelled in Daisy's direction towards the Yorkshire Dales where Lucy Weston lived in a beautiful old stone house on the edge of a small market town.

Daisy had spent many childhood holidays with her aunt when her parents were away on frequent and lengthy business trips. She'd always loved those visits and felt again the familiar childish excitement as she neared the house.

As she drove up to the door, Aunt Lucy came running out of the house, her face aglow with pleasure.

'My dear Daisy, it's so good to see you.'

She hugged her niece then held her at arms' length.

'Goodness me, I don't believe it, is this the same Daisy I saw in London those weeks ago? You look like my old friend again. You're alive at last. I am so pleased.'

'I must have looked terrible before.' Daisy laughed. 'But I do feel so much better and that's your doing. I can't thank you enough.'

Tears threatened to choke her voice.

'Tush, I don't look for thanks, you know that. Just to see you with a sparkle in your face is reward enough. We'll have a glass of wine to celebrate your rebirth. Bring your things in, usual room. I can't wait to hear all about your cottage and, of course, your grand business plan.'

Daisy hefted a briefcase from the back seat of her car.

'It's all in here, plus pictures of Elderflower Cottage. I hope you approve, both of cottage and plan, that is. The trouble is I keep thinking of all sorts of offshoots to the business. It's great to have my brain back, though whether or not it's got a business section I can't tell yet.'

'At least you have the potential background. Your father has certainly made his mark in the business world.'

'I hope it rubs off on me then.'

'You go unpack. I'll open the wine and then we'll just talk and talk.'

Talk they did, or rather Daisy did most of the talking while Lucy asked the questions. They sat in the garden until dusk, moved inside for supper, then talked on until Lucy called a halt just before midnight.

'Stop,' she cried. 'I can't take in one more fact or statistic, and as for cash flow analysis and building a website, how do you know all this?'

'I've had plenty of time, and maybe the idea of my own business was always there in my mind,' Daisy explained.

'I love the whole idea and it's a splendid plan — a herby heaven.'

'Herbiheaven.com — what a splendid name for my website, and it all started here, you know, Aunt Lucy. I first saw

Elderflower Cottage on a lovely June day and I remembered summer, coming here for the holidays, scents of lavender, marjoram, sage and that weird curry plant. You know the one, after sun and rain it smells just like an Indian restaurant. Suddenly I saw it, the future, growing and selling herbs, medical, culinary, cosmetic, information packs with each order, recipes, history, selling on the internet. There are stacks of outbuildings at Elderflower Cottage, one huge one I haven't even seen inside yet. And what about cooking with herbs?'

'You'd have to employ a cook. I can't see you tossing up lamb noisettes in tarragon and lemon cream sauce.'

'I can learn. Anything's possible in my new life. Why I can even . . . '

'No more,' Lucy said. 'Slow your brain or you'll never sleep.'

'I shall. I've got back the habit and especially after your supper and wine, and the relief at being able to get all this off my chest. People in the village are so curious about me and what I'm going to do at the cottage.'

'Can't you tell them?'

'No.'

'Why not? Is it a secret? From what you say if herbiheaven takes off, you'll be employing people, jobs in a rural area. Isn't that good?'

'I suppose I've lost the habit of trusting people after what happened.'

'You must find it again. You can't let that betrayal sour your life.'

'It won't, not now.'

'Any . . . er . . . friends you could talk to in the village?'

Lucy was so unusually diffident Daisy laughed.

'Men, do you mean?'

'Not specifically. I just . . . '

'You're too transparent. I know you're dying to get me settled with some suitable guy. Can't think why. You never married and you've a lovely life here. You had a great career.'

'Too late for me now so I have to live vicariously through my only niece.'

'You'll like Martha, my landlady, and her husband, Bob, and then there's Peter Macey.'

She glanced mischievously at Lucy.

'I do have a dinner date with him after I've moved.'

'A date! Tell me.'

'Oh, I think that's enough for one day. You'll never sleep, all this excitement, and I need to be sharp for tomorrow's meeting with the bank's financial adviser.'

'He'll be all right. His advice to me has always been spot on, but I want to help, too. I have plenty of spare cash looking for a good investment.'

'You've done enough for me. I have to do this by myself.'

The next few days were the happiest Daisy had known for months. Her aunt caught her enthusiasm and they lived, ate and slept herbs with Lucy's own well-stocked herb garden a practical starting point. On the last evening of Daisy's visit they even experimented with a recommended infusion of sage and thyme leaves to relax their throats aching from so much talk.

'Hm!' Aunt Lucy spluttered.

'Horrible!' Daisy grimaced. 'We haven't got that right. I think a glass of chilled white wine should take away the taste.'

'Good idea, but I do wish you weren't leaving. It's been so exciting for me,' Aunt Lucy said sadly.

'We're only at the beginning and I'm relying on you to help me. You'll come down?'

'Try stopping me, and I'll send down those bits and pieces of furniture that have been cluttering up my attic for years.'

'I'll enjoy having them,' Daisy said simply. 'What I'd do without you . . . '

'Mutual,' Aunt Lucy said gruffly, 'which brings me to an awkward matter. Your parents still don't know exactly where you are and it's getting harder and harder for me to stall them.'

'I'll write soon but I'm scared Dad'll come steaming down, pour cold water on my plans and make me go back to London.'

Lucy's heart contracted. The buoyant, confident young woman who'd so impressed the financial adviser, with her business plan intact, was again an uncertain child, unsure she was doing the right thing. She put her arms round her niece.

'You are absolutely on track, my dear, and I'm very proud of you. I'll deal with Edward but you must let them know your plans soon. Have confidence in yourself, keep in touch. Good luck.'

'Thanks.' Daisy said as she hugged her good-night. 'Thanks, thanks and endless thanks. You've been great. See you soon at Elderflower Cottage.'

Next day, Daisy drove westwards with a head full of plans, a car full of plant cuttings and most of Lucy's herbal library. She'd have to buy in to begin with but her plans were long term and increasingly ambitious.

Peter met her in the hotel carpark.

'Daisy, Martha told me you'd be back tonight. Great to see you. Let me help with those things. Plants?'

'Evidently.'

She took them from him.

'I'll just pop them into Bob's greenhouse.'

The old habit of secrecy closed around her as Peter took her case.

'Come and have a drink. The good news is that completion's on schedule. I'll meet you at the cottage first thing on Wednesday morning with the keys.'

'Peter, that's great news. I can hardly believe it. Let me buy you a drink, to celebrate. Mind you, it's practically supper time and I'm really hungry. Join me?'

'Well, I'd like to but . . . '

'OK, another time then.'

Irrationally, Daisy was a shade piqued. Peter seemed preoccupied, distant even. But then he'd done his job, the successful completion of the sale. Then he smiled.

'Why not? I'd love to. What a fool to

even think of turning down such an invitation. Let's have a good evening.'

And a good evening it turned out. For once The Skittish Pony was full, the bar very busy and a queue of people waiting for supper. Martha gave Daisy a quick hug.

'Good to have you back. Talk to you later. Peter joining you for supper? Good. Looks as though he could do with a good meal.'

Even Bob took time to call out, 'You've been away a long time. What'll you have? On the house.'

'You a local suddenly?' Peter said as he slid on to the bar stool next to her. 'Such preferential treatment.'

'It's nice.' Daisy smiled. 'Anyway, you seem to know most of the people in here. Who's that guy you were talking to by the window?'

'Geoff, my bodyguard.'

'What?'

'Just joking. Did you have a good time with your aunt? You look well.'

'Wonderful. We did a lot of work.'

'Work? What sort of work?'

Oh, no! She was so relaxed she'd nearly let her guard down.

'Oh, housework, tidying the garden. Aunt Lucy's got very bad arthritis,' she lied, crossing her fingers and offering up a silent apology to her very mobile aunt.

'Too bad, and when do your things arrive?'

'Things?'

'For the cottage. You do have furniture? I've fixed a van.'

'Well, no, I don't. I was going to Bathcombe tomorrow to buy a bed. Aunt Lucy's given me a few bits and she's sending down some other stuff.'

'Peter!'

A young man came over to the bar.

'Ages since I've seen you. Can you and your friend join us for a drink? We're over there.'

The stranger nodded pleasantly to Daisy.

'Hi, I'm Dan. Peter helped us with our house sale.'

Daisy soon found herself in a large group of people, having a thoroughly social evening and enjoying it. It was closing time before she knew it. Peter kissed her on the cheek at the door of the inn.

'Sorry we didn't get much chance to talk but you did promise to have dinner after the move. How about a week Saturday?'

She nodded.

'Fine. I'll look forward to it.'

'Good. See you Wednesday! D-Day.'

Bob bustled over.

'Come on, you two, you'll have my licence revoked.'

'By whom?' Peter scoffed. 'Nearest police station's at Bathcombe and that closes at five o'clock. I think you're pretty safe.'

'Go on then. Daisy needs her sleep.'

He gave Peter a friendly shove, slammed the door and shot the bolts.

It was only when Daisy was running her bath she remembered she hadn't asked Peter if it would be all right to camp at Elderflower Cottage the night before she moved in. Pouring in bath oil she reflected it couldn't possibly constitute a trespass and anyway who was to find out?

On the Tuesday, as she looked around her hotel room for the last time, Daisy felt a regretful pang. Empty of her belongings and impersonal now, it had been her path back to normality. The Skittish Pony had been a haven, Martha and Bob reassuring presences. The next day she'd be alone in Elderflower Cottage but it'd be home, her first true home. She shut the door and ran downstairs to return her key and say goodbye.

Martha and Bob looked worried.

'Bob says you should stay. He'll sleep in the snug and you can share my room. He says you shouldn't be camping alone out there and the weather forecast is terrible for later tonight.'

'Aye, you stay put,' Bob added.

'I wouldn't dream of taking your bed

110

but thanks for the offer. It's kind but actually I'm looking forward to it. I'll be back, and as soon as I have a cooker I hope you'll be over for supper. I need to experiment on you.'

'Experiment?'

Bob's eyebrows shot up in alarm.

'Oh, nothing, you'll see.'

Impulsively she kissed first Bob, then Martha.

'You've both been so kind. I've really felt at home here.'

'We'll miss you. I'd come with you but what with the new guests arriving any minute and a couple of busy weeks ahead . . . '

'I'll be fine, don't worry.'

Fortunately some advance members of the cycling group arrived at that point and Martha's and Bob's attention was diverted from Daisy. She skipped outside and drove off, apprehensive and elated at the same time. The apprehension vanished as soon as she reached the cottage. Bathed in evening sunlight it looked warm and welcoming. She walked round it, resisting the temptation to break in and take possession right away.

'Tomorrow,' she said as she patted the front door, then set about putting up her small, igloo-style tent.

Its brightly-coloured nylon looked strange tucked in a corner by the side of the old stone cottage. Martha had packed enough provisions for a week, including a flask of coffee and, joyful surprise, a bottle of red wine!

There were still a couple of hours of daylight and she pottered about the barn sorting out Aunt Lucy's plants. Dusk fell with remarkable suddenness as dark clouds rolled over the setting sun. The temperature dropped several degrees and Daisy was glad to zip herself into her tent and tackle Martha's picnic box. She lit the gas lamp and climbed into her sleeping-bag. It was cosy, a world apart. She sipped the wine and gave a sigh of satisfaction. Even in a tent in the garden it felt right to be near her new home.

Opening Aunt Lucy's copy of 'Culpepper's Herbal' she began to read and was soon absorbed in its fascinating snippets and recipes. A wind rippled the tent walls and spatters of rain began a light drumming. But then something different — a human voice calling her name.

'Daisy, Daisy Weston? Daisy, don't be alarmed it's only me, Jack. Are you all right?'

'Blast,' Daisy muttered, slithering out of her bag, knocking over her beaker of wine as she unzipped the doorway. 'What on earth are you doing here?' she said, trying not to sound cross.

'Just checking. There's going to be a storm tonight. Mother sent me to bring you to High Ridge. She was worried about you.'

He stooped and peered into the igloo.

'I can see you're pretty comfortable, though. Do you know you've spilled your wine?'

'Of course I do. I am very comfortable. It's very kind of Mrs Hawksworth to be concerned but the tent's water-proof. I was enjoying the peace.'

'Until I arrived?'

'I didn't say that.'

He eased himself into the tent which was hardly big enough to accommodate his broad, muscular body as well as Daisy. Thigh to thigh, Daisy was very conscious of him physically and tried to edge away. Jack merely reached across her to pick up the wine bottle.

'May I?'

He refilled her glass and passed it to her. She took a long swallow and passed it back to him. He took a drink.

'One of Bob's better ones,' he said appreciatively. 'Well, this is very friendly. I can see why you want to stay here but it really would be wiser to come back with me.'

His expression was warm and concerned, and Daisy was tempted. The wind blew harder, gusting around the tent, the gas lantern flickered and Jack's offer was appealing. Perhaps it was foolish to be out on what promised to be a very wild night.

Then remembered Helena and possibly Sonia would be at High Ridge.

'I really do want to stay here,' she decided.

'Do you want me to stay here with you?'

He said it as though the idea appealed greatly.

'Oh, no! Think of my reputation,' she joked, 'to say nothing of yours.'

'Who'd know?' he said softly.

'From my brief experience here, by morning most of the village would.'

'I could sleep across the tent flap,' he offered.

Daisy's pulse began to race. To her dismay she found she'd quite like him to stay. In a panic she manufactured a huge yawn.

'Please go, I'm tired. I'll be OK. I mean it.'

She leaned across him to unzip the tent. He caught her hand and pulled her nearer.

'You have your mobile?' he asked and

when she nodded he added, 'Take my number and phone me at any time in the night if you're worried. I'll be here in less than ten minutes.'

'You're making me nervous. What could happen?'

'Nothing, of course. It's just you're used to the city, lit streets, people, traffic. This is different. You should get a dog, invaluable in the country.'

'I'm going to get one as soon as I'm in the cottage.'

'Good. I'll look out for one for you. There are lots of farm puppies around and there's a pet rescue centre in Bathcombe. I'll come with you. Choosing a dog's a tricky business. Never had one?'

'No.'

'What you should look for is . . . '

'Jack, I do have my own ideas on the matter. Now please, go and let me get some sleep.'

He sighed.

'Well then, good-night, Daisy.'

The intention was to kiss her lightly

on the cheek but somehow as she turned towards him their lips touched, lingered, the kiss softening and deepening into a sweet sensation she had almost forgotten. For a few seconds she lost herself in its pleasure then drew away.

'You're sure you don't want me to stay?' he asked tenderly.

'I'm sure. Good-night, Jack.'

It was lonely without him but she was quite calm and relaxed. She was glad he'd been to check on her and it gave her a warm glow that someone should care enough. Gradually her eyelids fluttered, the book fell to the ground, she turned out the lamp and slept.

It was pitch dark when she woke later. The noise of wind and rain was ferocious and the tent shook under its buffeting but it wasn't the storm which had disturbed her. It was a door banging, a heavy door. It could be she'd left the barn door ajar. She thought she heard a dog bark, then the sound of vehicles. Fear prickled her scalp as she strained to listen.

Groping for her flashlight she touched the reassurance of her mobile phone. Jack had left his number, but she wouldn't use it yet. A flash of light swept through the tent — headlights? There was a crash of thunder, the door banged again and she felt sure she heard an engine start up. She waited for a few seconds then felt for her shoes. The tent was well hidden from the house so she could creep out to see if anyone was in the yard.

Very cautiously she peered out. The wind shrieked and rain plastered her hair to her skull within seconds. She drew back. It was ridiculous to go out in that. So far as she could make out there was nothing moving around the house. She couldn't see the outbuildings but there were no lights anywhere and no sounds apart from the gale. Creeping back into the warm sleeping-bag she resolved her first priority would be to get a dog!

7

The dawn chorus woke Daisy early. Crawling out of the igloo she breathed the pure cool air.

It was too early for Peter to arrive with the keys so she decided to take a walk. First she checked the back lane for possible tyre marks but the rain had obliterated any tracks there might have been.

Passing the outbuilding she did a double take. The padlock was not quite clicked into place and she was sure it had always been tightly closed. Undoing it she pushed open the door. She reached for the light switch and found the room was bare except for a large chest freezer by the end wall.

The lid was up and the freezer was empty but there were traces of ice and the bottom was very wet. It had been used quite recently. It wasn't very clean and there were dark reddish stains in one corner. The rattle of a sliding bolt brought her upright and she heard the padlock click.

'Hey,' she yelled running across the room, 'let me out.'

Hammering on the door she called out again until she heard footsteps outside and the door swung open.

'What the . . . '

'Peter! What on earth's going on?'

Peter, white-faced, was the more startled of the two.

'Daisy, do you realise it's not yet six o'clock? What were you doing in there? How did you get in?'

'It was unlocked, and where's all the farmer's stuff?'

Peter desperately tried to engage his brain in gear. It had been a hectic night with at most a couple of hours' sleep. He played for time.

'Why are you so early? I thought we said nine o'clock, after breakfast.'

'I forgot to tell you, I camped here last night, to be on the spot.'

120

'You were here, all night? In that storm anything could happen. No disturbances?'

'I thought I heard a vehicle of some sort but when I looked there was nothing.'

'You went out looking?'

'Only poked my head out. The rain forced me back.'

'It was insane to sleep outside on your own.'

'What's the problem? It's no big deal, one night camping out.'

'Because it could be dangerous is why. It was idiotic.'

'I thought the countryside was supposed to be safe. Anyway, why was the barn unlocked and why didn't you tell me the farmer had vacated it? And why's there a freezer there?'

Peter shut the door, padlocked it and handed her the key.

'I forgot to tell you. He moved out a week or so ago when you were visiting your aunt. He must have left it unlocked and we didn't notice. His wife probably used the freezer as an overflow for produce, big family.'

He dangled a set of keys before her.

'Now, do stop worrying. This is your big day, official occupation of Elderflower Cottage. Do you want me to carry you over the threshold?'

'I certainly don't, but I'll make coffee and there's enough food from Martha's box for a big breakfast.'

'Sounds ideal. And don't forget dinner with me next Saturday.'

A week later, it seemed to Daisy she'd never lived anywhere but Elderflower Cottage. It was more than habitable, cosy and comfortable with Aunt Lucy's few bits, substantial pieces which blended perfectly with the cottage's charm. Herbiheaven.com. was almost ready for a pilot launch to test the market and plants were on order ready for autumn planting. Joe Mitchell worked with her most days and was an absolute tower of strength.

She told him so one gusty summer

afternoon as they shared a coffee break in a sheltered corner of the garden.

'You've worked wonders, Joe. We're on schedule.'

'It's coming on.'

Joe's parents worked a smallholding near Bathcombe which was a precarious living and Joe was glad of extra work.

'What you really need is a heated greenhouse.'

'I know, I've thought about that. I'll see what's around.'

'Daisy,' he said, 'do we have to keep it secret?'

'What?'

'This business, herbiheaven. Folks are always asking what you're doing. Scared someone'll pinch the idea?'

'No. There are loads of people selling herbs but my herbiheaven is going to be the very best. Maybe I'm a bit cautious. I hope you'll be able to work full-time for me in the future.'

'I'd like that. Hey, here's a visitor. It's Mr Jack. I'll get on. Afternoon, Jack,'

Joe said and drained his coffee. 'What's this then?'

'This is for Daisy if she'd like it.'

Carefully he placed a black and white dog on the ground.

'Border Collie bitch, needed a kind owner. A friend of mine at the rescue centre brought her over. She's been ill treated but my friend swears she's sweet-natured. Come on, girl, say hello to Daisy.'

'She's lovely. How could anyone ill treat her?' Daisy exclaimed.

She kneeled and stroked her gently. The dog shrank away, ears laid back, then with a comical look of surprise she moved nearer, pushing her nose into Daisy's hand.

'I think she's perfect. Thank you. Has she a name?'

'They called her Sally after one of the centre's assistants. She was a stray, probably ran away from a bad owner. I'll give you her details, and Mother's sent over a food parcel, farm eggs and vegetables.'

'That's kind. I've had quite a few things left on my doorstep, jam, chutney, fruit, but I don't know who left them.'

'You'll find out.' Jack laughed. 'Village tradition. The anonymous welcome, it's called. When you're next in the village someone's bound to ask whether you enjoyed the jam or whatever and the next move will be up to you. You'll catch on, and by the way we'd like you to come to our end-of-season barbecue next Friday. Joe, you, too.'

'Brilliant. I was hoping you'd be asking.'

He turned to Daisy.

'It's the event of the year. You will go?'

'I don't think so. I'm really busy and I'm going out on Saturday.'

'Are you only allowed out one night a week? Something special?'

Jack's tone was over casual.

'Dinner date,' Daisy replied.

'I'll pick you up Friday,' Joe persuaded,

'then you can enjoy a glass or two of High Ridge cider. Come on, Daisy, you've worked so hard but you need to play, too.'

'I wouldn't like to leave Sally two nights running.'

'Bring her with you. Everyone's welcome, pets and all. We'll expect you both. You can get to know the door produce suppliers,' Jack added.

'We'll see,' she said.

Both she and Joe were busy every day sorting and planting and finally with some trepidation she launched herbi-heaven.com. on the prepared website and waited for something to happen. It did — with a vengeance. On the Friday morning of the barbecue she met Joe, waving a sheaf of e-mails.

'Look, Joe, orders, queries, lots. It's going to work. I'll get coffee then it's down to work.'

'Don't forget the barbecue. Starts at five, but it'll go on until late.'

'Oh, I couldn't, not now. There just isn't time.'

'You promised.'

'Maybe for a while then, if we go later.'

'Fine. We'll work through lunch,' Joe promised.

Later that evening, Joe picked them up in his battered old van. Daisy felt unaccountably nervous and held on tightly to Sally curled on her lap.

'It's very informal,' Joe said as he sensed her unease. 'Loads of people. You can lose yourself if you want to. Some of the year's visitors come back for it and there's one girl who came in the spring . . . '

'Ah! Now I see why you're so keen. Let's hope she turns up.'

'She will. Hayley's a girl of her word.'

Noise of music and laughter were already at high decibel level by the time Joe and Daisy arrived. Daisy looked in alarm at the milling crowd. She clutched Sally's lead tightly.

'Barbecue over there, dancing in the barn. Will you be all right for a bit while I look for Hayley?' Joe asked.

'Of course. I might want to leave . . . ' but Joe had disappeared.

She was considering setting off on the walk back when a plump, cheerful-looking woman came up to her.

'Hello, there, I hope you enjoyed the chutney I left. I'm Alice Matthews and I've a Border Collie, too. Perhaps we can walk them together one day. Shall I introduce you to people?'

'Thank you for the chutney. It was delicious.'

Alice grasped her arm.

'Come along then. Lots of people are dying to meet you.'

After half an hour, Daisy's head was spinning, meeting vicar, teachers, doctor, Women's Institute president and assorted others.

'Daisy,' she heard Jack's familiar voice with relief, 'is Alice giving you a hard time? There are some friends I want you to meet.'

'Mrs Matthews . . . er . . . Alice is being very kind,' Daisy replied.

Alice relinquished Daisy with a final,

'I'll telephone. We'll have a drinks party for you soon. There are still lots of folk you haven't met.'

Jack took Daisy's hand.

'You've not eaten, or had a drink?'

'Haven't had time.'

'You look great. Your hair. What have you done to it?'

'Nothing. It's grown quite a bit. Before I had it short.'

'Before,' he whispered softly, his mouth almost against her cheek. 'That elusive before. Daisy, the mystery girl, the girl with an unknown past.'

'Don't,' she snapped, though her heart was hammering at his closeness.

He noted her nervousness and changed tack.

'Sally settling?'

'Like a dream, more confident every day.'

'Good. Let's eat. Sally will be trampled to death in that crowd by the barbecue. In the orchard there's benches and tables. You grab one and I'll get some food and you can try our famous cider.'

Glad of the chance to be alone, Daisy wandered away from the main crowd towards the orchard where fairy lights were strung among the trees and seats were strategically placed for those who wanted a rest from the partying. She saw a few couples drawn together in earnest talk.

Sally settled down on the grass beneath a tree. Daisy undid her lead and joined her, leaning against the trunk. Closing her eyes her thoughts drifted.

'Mystery girl, secret pasts,' Jack had said.

Was it time to let go? Did it matter if people knew about herbiheaven? She couldn't possibly keep it secret much longer, and as for the other matter, she realised that living at Elderflower Cottage was beginning to erase the bad memories, even put them into clearer perspective, to accept she'd been only partially to blame for what happened.

The sound of clinking glass cut

through her thoughts. Good, Jack with supper. Maybe she'd confide in him. She turned her head and she made out two figures shadowed by dusk sitting on a bench partially screened by trees. She moved Sally's head and was about to get up when she heard her name.

'Daisy Watson, or is it Weston — she's causing some stir. Sonia told me Jack'll do anything to get his hands on that land, anything!' the voice went on. 'Already he's well in there. Bought her a dog. Sonia's mad about it all and as for Helena, well, she's just jumping.'

The two girls giggled, ice in glasses clinked.

'Attractive though, isn't she, Daisy Wotsit? My ma left a cake on her doorstep.'

'I wouldn't mind a crack at Jack Hawksworth myself except he's a bit elderly. Good luck with the Daisy woman, I say. Let's get another drink then we'll view the London talent and have a good gossip later.'

Daisy felt them pass within feet of her but they were so absorbed they noticed neither her nor Sally. Anger and disappointment overwhelmed her. Taken for a ride, again! Jack Hawksworth wasn't the least concerned about her, merely about her property, just as she'd originally suspected. No doubt he had some devious plan to oust her from Elderflower Cottage, but forewarned was forearmed.

As she emerged from the shadows she bumped into Joe and a group of young people.

'Daisy, I've found Hayley. She's brought some friends from London. Folks, this is Daisy Weston I was telling you about. Daisy, this is Hayley, Sam, Tessa, oh, you'll never remember their names. Come and have a dance. Isn't it a great party?'

'Not just now, Joe. I need to talk to Jack. He went to get some food.'

'He's in the barn. Sonia grabbed him.'

One of the girls was staring at Daisy.

'Don't I know you from somewhere? Your face is familiar. Were you in London before here?'

'No, no, it's not possible.'

Panic swept over her. She broke into a sweat then went ice cold.

'It'll come to me,' the girl persisted. 'Do you work in the media?'

'Joe, I . . . I don't feel too good. I'm going home. I'll find a lift, or I'll walk.'

All Daisy wanted was to be away from High Ridge and all these people.

'Take the van then. I can get a lift or kip down in the barn. I'd like to stay until the end.'

Joe handed her the keys. Daisy took them and put on Sally's lead. Head down, Daisy fled, reflecting bitterly only minutes ago she'd believed she'd come to terms with the past and was ready to put it behind her. And she'd been prepared to accept Jack Hawksworth was interested in her for her own sake!

'How could I be so stupid?' she said

as she crashed the gears of Joe's van. 'Not any more,' she vowed, driving away to the peaceful security of her own Elderflower Cottage, well away from prying eyes.

8

Daisy sat in the old-fashioned rocker Aunt Lucy had sent down and watched the flames leaping up the rough stone fireplace. The room glowed in the soft lamp and firelight. Relaxing music, a glass of wine and Sally at her feet slowly relaxed her as she recovered her senses.

She switched on her lap-top. E-mails, and the answerphone was blinking. She dealt first with the e-mails, orders, enquiries, and a peremptory demand from her father to let him know her whereabouts immediately.

'I will, I will, this weekend,' she promised herself.

Next she checked the phone. Disappointing — Aunt Lucy had sprained her ankle and would have to postpone her visit. Her heart missed a beat on the next message.

'Daisy, what on earth are you playing

at? Joe says you left in a hurry. I'll check you're home in five minutes, then I'm coming over.'

She took a sip of wine and stared at the telephone apprehensively. Suddenly, it rang.

'Ah, you're in. Why didn't you wait for supper? I was delayed.'

'Dancing in the barn with Sonia.'

'Who said that? She fetched me to fix the sound system and it took about ten minutes. I'll come for you and you can tell me your problem.'

'Don't patronise me, Jack. I'm very happy here. You go back to your party. Don't come here. I shan't answer the door if you do. Good-night.'

She switched off her lap-top well after midnight, tumbled into bed and overslept, only waking to the sound of Joe's rotavator outside. She made coffee and called him in.

' 'Morning, Daisy. Sorry about last night.'

She'd put last night behind her and didn't want to know if the girl with Joe had dredged up any memory about her. Work was the antidote to disconcerting thoughts and she and Joe put in a solid morning's work.

It was Joe who noticed the smartly-dressed man walking out of Bluebell Wood towards the house.

'This is private property,' Daisy called out. 'Are you lost?'

'Not exactly. I stopped to admire the view and lost the road. It's Elderflower Cottage and you must be Daisy Weston.'

'I am.'

'Is it about the greenhouse?'

'Greenhouse? Goodness, no, it's a personal matter.'

Daisy reluctantly stripped off her gardening gloves.

'I'm rather busy. Will it take long?'

'I shouldn't think so, and I'm sure you'll find my proposition well worth your time.'

The man's clothes were expensive, city style, no ordinary salesman this. Sally growled as he entered the house, sinking back on Daisy's command but keeping a belligerent eye on the stranger. He handed Daisy a card.

'Ray Bellings. I'm looking for a property.'

'There's a mistake,' Daisy said and handed back the card. 'This place isn't on the market. I've only just moved in.'

'I know that but my wife and I have been looking for a retirement home for two years. Six months ago we found Elderflower Cottage and instantly knew it was exactly what we wanted. It was empty then and not on the market. I was called abroad on urgent business and we were devastated when we came back to find it sold.'

'It must be a disappointment, but I'm sure you'll find somewhere else!'

'No, you don't understand, My wife has set her heart on this place. She's been quite ill and . . . '

'But it's not for sale,' Daisy insisted.

He named a figure which had Daisy reaching for the nearest chair. It was twice as much as she'd paid and spent on it.

'But that's crazy. It's not worth that.'

'It is to me, or rather, my wife. You see, I didn't want to bring this up but Judy, my wife, hasn't many years to live, and we've set our hearts on spending the rest of her time here. It is truly sad. So you see why . . . '

'Yes, yes, I do but . . . '

He held up his hand.

'Please, don't be hasty. Take time to think over my offer. I can see this has been a shock. Ring me this evening. My offer is genuine. I've written down the number of my bank on the card, and my financial adviser. Both will confirm my intentions. I look forward to your call. Meantime, may I give my wife hope?'

'No, I don't think you should,' Daisy said as she saw him out.

After he'd gone she sat watching Joe. Was she being cold-hearted and selfish? She reached for the phone.

'Hi, Aunt Lucy? How's the ankle?

Now listen to this . . . '

She ended the account of Ray Bellings' visit with, 'So should we at least think about it?'

'I think it sounds suspect. Can't you spot a phoney when one crosses your path? Phone him and tell him it's out of the question. No sale.'

'But just suppose it's genuine. You'd make a lot of money.'

'I don't want a lot of money. I want your peace of mind, and your website's stunning. I put in an order just now. Everything else OK?'

'Fine. So disappointed you can't come yet.'

'Don't worry, I'll get there. And don't forget, Daisy, no sale!'

Daisy rang off, relieved, but worried because she had almost fallen for the stranger's story. She decided to tell Peter about the man when they went out for dinner that night but when she finally came indoors there was a message on her answerphone calling off the date.

'So sorry, Daisy. Something really urgent's cropped up and I have to be away. Maybe next week? Talk to you later.'

Peter's voice sounded strained. He'd seemed worried lately, jumpy and uneasy. She phoned him and left a message on his answerphone.

'Fine, I'll look forward to next week.'

For the rest of the day she became absorbed in her website and forgot all about Ray Bellings, but he arrived at her door early next day before Joe turned up. His manner was decidedly less charming than before.

'You didn't ring,' he accused.

'I'm sorry, I was working, but the answer is the same. I'm not selling.'

'How am I to tell my poor wife? Our hearts are set on this place and when I'm set on something, Miss Weston, I don't give up easily.'

'I've said no, so there's no point. Look, there's an estate agent in Bathcombe, Peter Macey.'

'Thanks, I already know Macey. I wouldn't deal with him if he was the last estate agent in the country, and it's this place I want. I do urge you to reconsider.'

He pushed the door wider and made to come into the cottage.

'No, it's pointless. I am not selling.'

She tried to close the door on him but he only pushed harder.

'No,' she cried out, alarmed by his attitude, 'you can't!'

Sally hurled herself forward, teeth bared, but Ray Bellings beat a hasty retreat to his car. Daisy watched him slam the door and switch on his mobile to make what, from his body language, was a very angry call. She shivered as she went to make coffee.

She tried to forget the incident but the unpleasant memory lingered and she was glad Joe had promised to come in for a few hours even though it was Sunday. However, Jack Hawksworth arrived before him.

'Aren't you busy?' she asked coldly.

'I am but I wanted an explanation as to why you left in such a rush Friday night. A bit melodramatic.'

'Melodramatic? Maybe that fits with your own consummate bit of acting, pretending you've no interest in my land whilst all the time you're planning ways to get hold of it. Well, you won't, especially now your intentions are quite clear.'

'What are you on about? I told you we've accepted the situation. It's no big deal, and there are other areas of expansion. Whom did you talk to on Friday? Why can't you be honest and tell me what you heard?'

'I heard the truth,' she snapped, 'so don't deny it.'

'Deny what? Your trouble, Daisy, is some sort of persecution complex. You are paranoid about some event in your past you can't deal with. Did you harm someone, steal or embezzle company funds? Is that why you're so secretive about your past and your future? Even all this here is supposed to be secret when everyone knows you're establishing a herb nursery. For goodness' sake, I even found your website last night, and it's great.'

'Who told you? Joe?'

At that point Joe himself arrived by bicycle. She rounded on him.

'You told, didn't you? I trusted you.'

'Hold on, Daisy. Told what?' Joe asked.

'The herbs, what we're doing.'

'I never did,' he said simply. 'I promised.'

'Oh, come on,' Jack said, 'Joe didn't tell anyone, but it doesn't take a great brain. You ordered a greenhouse from Gardenscape, and two people from the village work there. Then there's loads of plant delivery vans with horticultural logos, postmen with endless catalogues. Why don't you want people to know you're trying to set up a herb business? It's not illegal.'

'It's no-one's business but mine.'

'If you live in the country,' Jack said patiently, 'you have to put up with a certain amount of nosiness. I've told you before. Why can't you accept it?'

'Because I can't.'

Hurt pride, annoyance, disappointment, Jack's betrayal, all drove her to unreasonable anger.

'And because I don't want my affairs raked over and gossiped about.'

She turned to Joe.

'And I expect it's all over the village now that that girl with you recognised me. The court case should give them something to chew over.'

'What court case?' Jack asked.

'She didn't recognise you. As soon as you left she forgot all about it. It was a party, Daisy,' Joe blurted out.

'What court case?' Jack insisted, looking at her strangely.

'Just go away, both of you.'

She knew she sounded childish but it was the only way she could think of to escape the questions. It was turning out to be a real black Sunday.

'I only came to work. I don't care what happened in the past. It's now I'm concerned about,' Joe said and went to the barn to get his tools.

Jack shook his head and made to move towards Daisy, then stopped.

'OK, I'm going, but I will just say it's a shame to spoil what you're doing so well here, by being blinkered by paranoia and blind stupidity.'

He strode angrily away and drove off with screeching tyres leaving Daisy on her own as she'd demanded. She felt no sense of achievement at all.

Looking back, Daisy saw the night of the barbeque as the beginning of a campaign. That overheard bit of gossip might been have been deliberately carried out. She was never to find that out but events quickly followed which clearly pointed to a burning desire on someone's part to oust her from Elderflower Cottage.

A couple of days later she came downstairs to a glum-faced Joe.

'Here, Daisy, I hope you don't mind, I've made your coffee. I think you're going to need it. All the young plants in the experimental plot . . . '

'What? Quickly, tell me.'

'Ruined! Sheep are in, had a right feast, and what they haven't eaten they've trampled to death. I reckon we can save only about five per cent of the plants.'

'Sheep? But how and from where?'

'Must be High Ridge. Gate to their top field was wide open and they're all over the place.'

'High Ridge? But the sheep are mostly at the other side of the farm.'

'Usually, but something must have happened. Whatever it was our first sowing's lost. What'll we do?'

'Do? We get those animals out. Save what you can and I'll re-order right now. I'll have the nursery send replacements by express.'

'I think I'll call High Ridge first,' Daisy said grimly, and headed for the phone, dialling the number.

'High Ridge. Helena Hawksworth,' the voice answered — Helena!

'Daisy Weston here. Will you please

arrange to remove your sheep from my land?'

'Sheep? How do you know they're ours? Lots of sheep on the moors.'

'Because your gate was left open, accidentally or on purpose, but whatever, I expect payment for the damage they've caused.'

Helena's laugh was bitterly spiteful.

'You'll be lucky. Sheep have a right to wander the moor and if you had any sense you'd have taken your own precautions to fence off the property. Your land's an extension of High Ridge anyway. Those dotty sisters wheedled it out of my grandfather. It should have come to me. You won't last five . . . hey, don't . . . '

The phone was evidently snatched away from her and Jack spoke.

'Daisy, what's the trouble?'

'Your sheep, my first planting, your sister.'

'I'll be right there.'

The phone went dead. By the time he arrived, most of the sheep had wandered back across the moor to High Ridge but two or three evaded Joe's waving arms and Sally's amateurish but delighted attempts to round them up against a wall.

'Oh, no!' Jack exclaimed when he saw the damage. 'I can't understand it. I shut that gate myself. Last night, there was a ewe on her back, couldn't get up. It was late and I was patrolling the farm. We've had sheep stolen lately. The gate was closed then. I'm certain of it.'

He looked so upset Daisy could almost believe he was genuine.

'Look, of course we'll pay compensation. Take no notice of what Helena said. Let me handle this.'

Within seconds, he had the sheep in his trailer and was assessing the damage.

'A lot of this can be salvaged if you work fast. I'll send Donna and Tim down. Work on the complex is tailing off and there's still a couple of weeks before they go back to college. They'll be glad to help.'

Daisy looked doubtful. Extra hands would be a help, but Hawksworths' hands? But she liked the twins who seemed totally free from any design on Elderflower Cottage. She'd met them a couple of times and they'd been as charming and friendly as their mother. Jack put his arm round her shoulder.

'Cheer up, Daisy, it's not too bad. I don't know how it happened and I'm sorry for the other morning, too. We shouldn't quarrel. We're on the same side, and should work together.'

He turned her to face him, his dark eyes searching hers, warm, friendly, asking for her trust. But she'd seen that look once before.

Then, the eyes were blue and he wasn't a farmer but a top consultant at a London teaching hospital. She'd given him her trust which he'd instantly betrayed. Was it possible to trust this man in front of her who also protested he had her welfare at heart?

They were very close and he was drawing her closer, both arms around her and her treacherous body nearly yielded. Then she remembered those words in the orchard on the night of the barbeque.

'Jack'd do anything to get his hands on that land, anything.'

She pushed him away and said coolly, 'I don't think that would do. You see, I don't believe you, Jack, and I certainly don't trust you.'

9

As Daisy put the finishing touches to her make-up, the doorbell rang. She was looking forward to dinner with Peter. The business was going well and she'd finally told her parents her plans and invited them down to stay.

Peter gave her a bunch of flowers and kissed her cheek when she opened the cottage door to him.

'Thanks, they're lovely. I'll put them in water then I'm ready. Where are we going?' she asked.

'Pub with restaurant the other side of Exeter. Quite a drive but worth it.'

'OK,' she said and bent to give Sally a hug. 'You're on guard.'

The days were shortening as autumn approached and they crossed the moor in deepening purple twilight.

'Here we are,' he said after a while. 'The Fig and Olive. Just enough light left for you to see what a pretty place it is.'

As he drove round the back of the pub looking for a parking place Daisy's attention was drawn to a man sitting in his car.

'Peter, that man over there, isn't it the man who was in The Skittish Pony that night your friends were in?'

'Where?' he asked sharply as he drew into a parking space.

He hardly glanced in the direction indicated before coming round to open the door for her, never mentioning the man in the car.

'We'd better go in. I booked for eight o'clock and it's well past.'

He grasped her arm and hustled her into the pub.

Daisy enjoyed the evening. The atmosphere was relaxed and friendly and the food and wine excellent. Peter seemed more at ease, too, less jumpy than of late. The only jarring note came when she told him about Ray Bellings' visits.

'I gave him your name. Has he been in touch about a property?' she asked.

'No. What did he look like?'

'Smart, expensive, new car, city type.'

'Did he leave a card?'

'Yes, he did. I think it's in my bag. Yes, here.'

She handed it to him. Peter frowned.

'It's worth checking him out. It was a crazy price to offer for Elderflower Cottage. I doubt the wife exists. It's an old ploy to soften a vendor's heart, but don't worry about him. He's unlikely to visit you again.'

But Peter himself was worried. He didn't like the sound of it, nor Daisy's account of the sheep and ruined plants. She'd told him all about her business over dinner. He was thoroughly impressed by her progress.

The moonlit drive back across the moor was entrancing but as Peter was about to turn off the main road Daisy noticed two cars in a lay-by. Both headlights on and two men were leaning against the bonnet of the first car. It was a momentary image but there was something familiar about one of the men. It teased her brain but she forgot it as the lights of Elderflower Cottage beamed out to greet them.

'You left a lot of lights on,' Peter remarked. 'I hope you're going to invite me in for coffee.'

'Sure, it's been such a nice evening, but, Peter, I didn't leave all those lights on, just the hall and porch.'

Anxiety gripped her as she realised something was missing. The house was too quiet. Sally always made a great to-do of either barking a welcome or warning.

'Something's wrong,' she said tersely. 'No Sally, too many lights.'

Peter jumped out of the car and ran up to the front door. It was half-open. Very cautiously he pushed it. Daisy was right behind him.

'Shh,' he hissed, 'someone's been here. I think they've gone, but stay back, just in case.'

He stepped inside, into the living-room and groaned.

'Oh, no, you've been burgled.'

'Where's Sally?'

Daisy was becoming increasingly frantic.

'Oh, no,' she exclaimed as she came into the room. 'Where's Sally?'

'Probably outside. The front door was open.'

'But she'd come back as soon as I got here.'

She dashed out into the garden, calling for her dog, while Peter phoned the police before coming out to help. Daisy was yelling the dog's name.

'Shh, she's not here. She might be locked up. Listen.'

He put a hand on Daisy's arm to quieten her. From inside the cottage a faint, distressed whine sent Daisy hurtling back inside.

'Upstairs,' Peter said. 'Bathroom,' he said.

The whining became louder, desperate, as Daisy tried to open the door.

'Locked, no key here. Peter, please, break it down.'

'No need for that.'

He pulled a piece of plastic from his pocket and deftly jiggled it through the door. Daisy called out reassurance to the dog until they were inside. Sally lay by the door, panting for breath, obviously hurt but still able to give her tail a thump as Daisy kneeled by her, running expert hands over her. She checked for a pulse and flashed a small torch in the dog's eyes.

'Bruised but not broken,' she said tersely, 'and if ever I find out . . . '

She felt Sally's ribs carefully but a yelp of pain stopped her.

'Someone's kicked her. There may be some ribs broken. I'll strap her up and give her a tranquilliser.'

Peter watched, puzzled.

'You're not a vet, are you? That was all very professional.'

'What? 'Course not. Basic first aid. Could you help me carry her downstairs to her basket and then we'll look at the other damage? Main thing is Sally will be OK.'

The sound of a car outside made Sally flinch.

'Police probably.'

The police checked the house over. The bedrooms were largely undisturbed but the TV and the music centre had gone. The velvet sitting-room curtains had been pulled down and furniture was overturned.

'A couple of tramps used to doss down here in the winter,' one of the officers said. 'They probably came by all prepared to settle in, saw it occupied and did a bit of spiteful damage and petty thieving. I doubt if you'll see your things again.'

'My computer!'

Daisy had been too concerned about Sally to worry overmuch about her material possessions but so much of business was on the computer, some backed up, some not.

'Looks like that's vanished, too,' the other officer said. 'Much on it?'

'Loads. Hours and hours of work.'

'We'll do our best, miss. You've not lived here long, I believe. Settled in all right? Any . . . er . . . enemies? Anyone likely to have a grudge?'

The senior officer spoke casually but his colleague still had pencil poised.

'Any strangers call recently?'

'No. People have been very friendly except . . . '

'Except?'

'Oh, it's nothing really.'

Helena Hawksworth obviously bitterly resented her being at Elderflower Cottage but somehow she couldn't see Helena or Jack kicking Sally.

'I did have someone round last week, very odd.'

She told them about Ray Bellings.

'My friend here was going to check on him. He has Bellings' card.'

'We'll take care of that, sir.'

The officer held out his hand to Peter. Reluctantly Peter handed over the card, and after a few more sympathetic noises the officers left, promising to report any developments. Peter made coffee, Daisy found a bottle of brandy and with Sally settled as comfortably as possible sat down to recover from the shock. Peter re-hung the curtains and tidied up the room before joining her.

'I'm sorry, Daisy, it's rotten luck. You don't deserve it.'

'Do you think someone's trying to tell me something, Peter?'

'Hope not,' he said, hoping his voice was more convincing than he felt.

The next few weeks were uneventful, marked mainly by the frustrations and sheer hard slog of setting up a new computer and checking through all the herbiheaven data. Sally recovered rapidly from a couple of cracked ribs and Martha insisted Daisy had an alarm system fitted and Peter, of course, knew the very man to fit it. Jack Hawksworth, still angry, made a formal, brief visit.

One annoying consequence of the burglary was Daisy's phone had gone haywire. She was plagued with wrong numbers, phantom callers who never spoke. In the end she bought a new phone and changed her number and life began to return to normal — until Alice Matthews' Hallowe'en party.

Alice had been very kind after the burglary even helping Daisy with some of the computer work so it was impossible to refuse the invitation even if she'd wanted to. She asked if Sally could come, too. The day of Hallowe'en was crisp and sunny.

Joe and Daisy worked out of doors on the lay-out of a flagged exhibition herb garden and Daisy worked on long after Joe had gone home, oblivious of time passing until a chill in the air told her the day was practically over. Alice's party started in an hour, she realised, and she was nowhere near ready. Sally needed a good walk first, so she went indoors, checked the computer, dealt with some new e-mails and called Sally.

The wood would have to do. Daisy needed a bath and time to put on something partyish. There was still some daylight left but once in the woods darkness seemed to fall quickly. After half an hour Daisy decided to call it a day. It was now quite dark.

'Sally,' she called, relieved at the instant rustlings that showed her dog was nearby. 'Home, girl. Come on.'

Something large and black suddenly swooped down on her, knocking her to the ground. Shrieks and yells sounded all around her. She tried to get up but something pinned her down and there was a blow to her head. Something sharp grazed her cheek and she felt blood trickle down her face. She glimpsed shapes, some in white, some dark, all around her. Chants and yells mocked her, fingers poked at her.

'Out, out. Witch, witch, fly away on your broomstick.'

'All right,' she gasped. 'Not a nice trick-and-treat at all. Let me up now.'

Kids and Hallowe'en! She should have known better than to venture into the wood, but an uneasy fear began to grip her. These weren't young children. The voices were adolescent, and there was a smell of alcohol.

'Let me up,' she shouted. 'I've got my mobile and if you don't stop I'm calling the police.'

She fumbled in her jeans pocket but the others were faster.

'Got your mobile, got your mobile, witch's mobile.'

It was snatched from her and to her horror she felt a rope thrown round her waist.

'Stop it, stop it.'

She tried to strike out but the hands holding her were strong. She heard the distant sound of smashing glass and knew her greenhouse was being vandalised. Now she began to fight in earnest, kicking out and yelling at the top of her voice but she was severely outnumbered.

'Tie the witch up, tether her to that tree.'

A rough, excited male voice rose above the rest and she was jostled and half-dragged through the trees. She'd almost given up hope when the wonderfully welcome sound of snarling yelps and barks rang out.

'Sally,' she yelled but it wasn't only Sally.

Two large beasts hurled themselves into the group surrounding her and at the same time shots rang out. More shots were fired and a familiar voice full of fury roared out.

'Get away, you lunatics. Catch them, Leo, don't let them get away. Daisy, it's all right.'

And there was Jack Hawksworth laying about them with a stick. There was a sound of snapping teeth and the voice of a terrified youth.

'Meant no 'arm . . . just to frighten . . . call off your dog.'

Then the shapes ran, stumbling, howling as Leo and Sally chased after them. Jack rushed over to Daisy and held her tightly to him.

'It's OK. OK. They're just kids going too far. I'll call off the dogs in a minute but they deserve a good fright. You hurt?'

'No, just scared witless. They'd been drinking, Jack, Who are they?'

'Not kids from the village, that's for certain. I recognised a couple of yobs from Southcross. We've had trouble with them before.'

'Why me? Someone's out to scare me away from here. If you hadn't come along Sally could never have tackled that lot. They'd've killed her.'

'She was doing pretty well when I did come along. I was right over by the stream when I heard the commotion. Luckily it's a still night and the racket carried. Let's get you back to the cottage. Can you walk?'

'I think so . . . ah! No, seems not. I think my ankle's twisted.'

'Good excuse to carry you.'

He swung his gun round his shoulders, dropped his stick, gave a piercing whistle and picked up Daisy easily. He held her firmly to his chest and Daisy was just pleased to be there. They soon reached the cottage.

'Don't look at the greenhouse. It looks worse than it is and won't take long to put right. Now, we'd better ring Alice. I don't think either of us is fit for a party.'

'You can go. I'll be all right.'

'Wouldn't dream of it. I'd much prefer to spend the evening with you.'

She was happy to let Jack take charge. She was sore and bruised with a cut on her cheek and a swollen right ankle. Jack bathed her face, propped her foot on a stool and phoned Alice to tell her what had happened.

'Everyone is concerned and Martha is coming over to spend the night here,' he said once he'd hung up.

'That's very kind but really there's no need. I don't think they'll be back.'

'We'd all feel happier if someone was with you. I'll light the fire and make us supper. Just relax.'

'How can I? It was scary, and what about the next time? Someone wants me out of here and I'm beginning to wonder if it's worth staying. I should have taken that man's offer.'

'What offer?' Jack asked.

She told him about Ray Bellings' visits and his extraordinary high offer.

'Stranger and stranger. But you must realise by now that I'm not after your land. It isn't worth anything like that and we couldn't afford that sort of money anyway.'

'Who is it then?'

'I don't know. Let's eat, talk later.'

In a remarkably short time Jack came back from the kitchen with a tray.

'Salad, herb omelette, and I found a bottle of white wine in the fridge.'

'I'm not much of a cook although I love food,' she said.

'Anyone can make an omelette.'

'I can't but I'm willing to learn.'

'I'll come round and cook a real meal for you one day. Organic High Ridge rack of lamb with rosemary and garlic's my speciality.'

She stared in amazement at Jack. She'd classed him as the rugged, outdoor farmer who'd be unlikely to know how to boil an egg, but the omelette was perfection and the salad had a delicate herb dressing too individually tasty to be out of a bottle. He put down his fork and looked at her, mouth curving in amusement at her expression.

'I know just what you're thinking — outdoor man, couldn't boil an egg. You made a snap judgement in Bluebell Wood, didn't you?' he said.

'I suppose I did.'

'You still think that?'

He got up, came over and took her hands in his. She shook her head.

'Well, I have to confess I took you for a tough city girl who hadn't a clue about rural life.'

'I grant you the second part but I'm anything but tough.'

'I see that now. You're a vulnerable woman who's been badly hurt by someone or something in the past. I know you'll tell me about it when you're ready and you'll see it doesn't

168

matter any more. Here and now is what matters and I'm not going to let you leave Elderflower Cottage.'

It was the most natural thing for Jack to bend to kiss her and she put her arms around his neck and kissed him back. Jack then spoke softly.

'I promise you it'll come right. Trust me.'

Daisy hesitated. Could she trust Jack? She'd little choice. She needed his help to remain in the village, and she desperately wanted to stay.

'I will,' she said and raised her face to his again, relaxed and secure.

It was much later when Jack finally left, with Martha settled in the spare room, that Daisy had a sudden flash of recall. Relaxed, sleepy, thinking of Jack, she suddenly saw the image of the man leaning on the bonnet of the car in the lay-by near her cottage, and she was sure she knew who he was.

10

'What a novelty, me getting breakfast for you,' Daisy said and spooned a couple of boiled eggs out of the pan.

'It's a treat for me to be waited on. Coffee's excellent,' Martha replied. 'How are you feeling this morning? What a blessing Jack turned up.'

'Yes, fortunately for me it seems to be a habit of his. Can I ask you something? Jack, is he . . . um . . . he and Sonia . . . you know?'

'Not as far as I know. He took her to young farmers' dos ages ago and gossip says Sonia's still keen, but Jack's not playing. I think you've put her nose out of joint where Jack's concerned.'

'Oh, dear. You don't think she had anything to do with last night?'

'No, no, she wouldn't go to those lengths. Don't despair. Jack's ferreting around, Bob, too. We all like you and we'd like to keep you.'

'I'm glad. I want to stay, but I'm beginning to suspect everybody, even Peter. There's a guy keeps turning up when Peter's around, big bloke, earrings, very dark. He was in The Skittish Pony that night with Peter's friends and I'm sure he was in the carpark in the Fig and Olive hotel Peter took me to last night, then later in the lay-by near the lane. He could have burgled Elderflower Cottage while Peter kept me away having dinner.'

'What would Peter gain from that? Peter has his problems but I do know he wouldn't harm you for anything. He's fond of you.'

'I like him, too, but I just don't know whom or what to believe.'

Daisy had lots of visitors that day bearing sympathy and comfort tokens, flowers, cakes, jams, and enough chutney to set up a small market stall! Jack didn't ring that day, or the next. Although she had plenty to occupy her Jack would keep creeping back into her thoughts, but as the days passed with no word from him she began to regret returning his kisses.

Jack was, in fact, busy travelling the county, not only picking up information on Daisy's behalf, but on another problem. The police seemed powerless to prevent increasing numbers of sheep being spirited away from the remote moors. A surprising whisper reached his ears which he was duty bound to check out. He tackled Peter Macey in his office, first making sure Sonia wasn't there.

'I'm astonished to discover that your name has been passed along as being behind the sheep-stealing racket,' he accused.

Peter's laugh was genuine.

'Who said that? I don't know one end of a sheep from another.'

'You don't need to, and you're an expert on . . . er . . . processing goods.'

'Maybe, but not sheep. I've a good idea who is behind it and why my name's been given.'

'Who?'

'I'm in enough trouble without laying my neck on another chopping block. The men you're after are professional villains, not amateurs like me.'

'The other matter is Daisy's harassment. Anything to do with you?'

'Definitely not. I like Daisy far too much. Why would I want her out?'

'Rumour says you've a lot of fingers in some unsavoury pies. There could be a connection.'

'I'll be honest. I sold Daisy the cottage on impulse, to get me out of a small difficulty. It's brought me nothing but trouble since, but I can guess who's trying to get her out.'

His mobile bleeped, he listened, nodded then switched off.

'Got to go, sorry, urgent. Catch you later.'

He ushered Jack out of his office, leaped into his car and roared off.

He called Jack later that evening.

'Sorry about this morning. I need to talk to you. I'm leaving here for a while but it's urgent we warn Daisy. I think something bad's to happen soon. Can you be at the Feathers in half an hour? I'll know more then.'

'Half an hour's pushing it but I'll do my best.'

Jack intended to ring Daisy but a long phone call from his accountant delayed him. It was well over half an hour before he arrived at the Feathers. The carpark was full, but there were further spaces at the rear. As he left his car, he heard muffled cries. He turned round and saw two men dressed in boiler suits and black balaclavas punching someone on the ground.

Jack launched himself at one of the men, shouting for help.

'OK,' one of them shouted. 'That'll do, he'll have half the pub out. Go, go, take his car.'

With a last kick at the prone figure the men leaped into a car. Jack tried to stop them but was pushed away violently before the car screamed out of the carpark and on to the main road.

He bent to examine the man who was painfully getting to his feet.

'Peter!'

'Jack, thank goodness it's you. I think those thugs were out to kill or cripple me and if you hadn't arrived . . . '

'Looks like they've taken your car, too. Are you badly hurt? We should phone the police.'

'Not yet. Into your car before people come out to see what's happening. Please, Jack. It's vital. We have to get to Daisy. I'm all right. Just drive.'

Daisy's heart leaped as she opened the door but her smile vanished when she saw Peter's blood-stained face. Her response was automatic. She reached out for Peter, and with Jack took him into the sitting-room.

'Lie quite still. I'll get my bag. Jack, warm water, towels in the drawer.'

She felt Peter's pulse then ran her hands over neck, ribs and stomach.

'Not too bad. Let's see the head. You've bled a lot. How do you feel?'

'OK. Jack turned up just in time.'

'It's a nasty gash. I'll clean it up.'

Both men looked amazed as she rummaged in the bag where she'd kept a few emergency things. Now she was glad she hadn't thrown it all out. As her training took over, Jack looked at the initials on the black bag, D.A.W.

'Yours?'

'Of course.'

She was dabbing something on Peter's face.

'Nasty bruises. You'll look a mess tomorrow and you may have a couple of cracked ribs. You need an X-ray. We should take you to hospital.'

'You're a doctor!' Jack exclaimed.

'Let's get Peter sorted first. I'll ring the hospital.'

'No.'

Peter sat up and winced. At that moment Sally sat up, barking. Jack ran over to the window and pulled back the curtains. Smoke and flames billowed into the night sky.

'The barn,' Daisy gasped. 'All my stuff's in there.'

Jack was already dialling emergency.

'I knew something like this was planned. I'm sorry, Daisy,' Peter groaned.

But she was already outside closely followed by Jack who grabbed her arm and pulled her away from the blazing building.

'Don't be a fool. It'll be an inferno in there.'

He put his arms round her.

'Not worth it. You can't get in there now and the fire brigade should stop it spreading to the other buildings. Come back inside. I think Peter has some explaining to do, as you do, Doctor Weston.'

'I can't go in and just sit and watch my stock burn. Is this going to go on until I'm forced out?'

'That's what we may find out from Peter, before the fire brigade arrives.'

Head in hands, Peter was staring gloomily into the sitting-room fire.

'All my fault. I shouldn't have pushed you into buying this cottage.'

'You didn't, I wanted it. I just want all this to stop. It's horrible.'

'If it's any consolation this is the end of it. I've been to the police. They know everything. They'll probably arrive with the fire brigade.'

'So tell us,' Jack said, 'before they get here.'

Peter sighed.

'I did push Daisy into buying the cottage because I needed it and couldn't afford to buy it. I used it as my headquarters, I suppose. It's well off the beaten track and ideal for storing various things.'

'Things? What things?' Daisy asked in amazement.

'I can't pussyfoot around any more. I have to confess. Daisy, Jack, I'm a bad lot. I've broken the law, upset some powerful people. I was going to leave the country quietly, live in Australia, but I had to stop what was happening to you first.'

'I can't believe you're a bad lot,' Daisy said.

'I started small-time, organised poaching, trout, game, good market in the cities. But never sheep or cattle,' he said to Jack. 'One thing led to another. Antique dealers wanted tip-offs about country estates coming on the market. I began to handle a few stolen pieces. I started to hang out with real villains and then . . . well, I got into smuggling. Tobacco, cigarettes from the Continent, van loads, a team of drivers, making contacts — a big-time operation and very profitable. We used to meet here, using Elderflower Cottage as a warehouse and contact point. All at night, of course.'

'Wasn't it a bit drastic to sell this cottage to Daisy?'

'It just seemed right at the time, and I really liked Daisy. I wanted her to have Elderflower Cottage, she was so keen. I thought I'd continue to use it until something turned up and in the end I found an old warehouse near Bristol. We shifted everything the night you camped out. Frightened me to death when I found you in there.'

'The freezer? That always puzzled me.'

'Trout, pheasants, salmon.'

'But it doesn't explain what's happening out there. Surely you aren't trying to get me out.'

' 'Course that wasn't me but there is a connection. If I hadn't sold the cottage to you, Tim Burden, the real villain, would have got it. He was furious with me over that, swore to get his own back.'

'Tim Burden, who's he?' Daisy asked, puzzled.

'A very shady property dealer. He was desperate for Elderflower Cottage because he pays officials well for any tit-bits of confidential information regarding planning development and his mole told him your land was earmarked in the next couple of years for an estate of low-density, very expensive executive homes and if that happened this place and its ten acres would be worth a fortune.'

'They'd never get permission,' Jack exploded.

'Burden was willing to pay back-handers to anyone of influence on the council but they won't now because I've told the police all I know about Burden and his dealings. They're after him for tax and VAT fraud anyway.'

'And Ray Bellings?'

'One of his partners, with no sick wife. That first attempt didn't work so he enlisted a few helpers, wild youngsters, to try and scare you off.'

'The burglary?'

'A couple of lads from Southcross.'

'That guy in The Skittish Pony the other night, and in the lay-by on the night of the burglary?'

'Geoff? Nothing to do with Burden. He's one of the good guys. He appointed himself my official minder. He knew what Burden was planning for me. Unfortunately he went off duty tonight. Oh, that sounds like the fire engine. I should put the kettle on, Daisy. Thirsty work, putting out a fire.'

She went over and took his hand.

'Peter, I'm so sorry, but I still don't believe you're really a bad lot. When this is all over, what you need is a fresh start. I'll be here if you need me.'

'You'll visit me in prison?'

'If that's necessary. Can't afford to lose a good friend.'

Hours later, Elderflower Cottage was again quiet. The barn smouldered and not much had been salvaged but the fire had been prevented from spreading to other buildings. A cursory examination pointed to arson and the whole business was now under police investigation. A police car had taken Peter to hospital.

'Quite a night,' Daisy said. 'Poor Peter. What'll happen to him, Jack?'

'I don't know. It's a complicated business. He's weak, not bad. What he didn't tell you is he has a gambling problem and that was the start of it, that and a taste for risk-taking. One and the same thing, I suppose. He was in debt, too, that's why he couldn't buy

Elderflower Cottage himself. But it's you I want to talk about, Doctor Daisy. Why make such a mystery of that?'

She took a deep breath. Time to lay down that demon at last.

'Twelve months ago, I was involved in a court case, in connection with a baby's death. It was a high-profile case as the parents were well-known. They sued the hospital and won punitive damages. Sadly, the baby would have died anyway but the prosecution found the hospital negligent. I was officially in charge but when I saw how the birth was going I called in my superior consultant. He never arrived, the baby died, and the consultant denied I'd ever called him. It was his word against mine.'

'And why didn't he back you up?'

'To save his reputation, I assume. He never spoke to me after it happened. Like a fool, I trusted him. He's a brilliant surgeon, brings lots of research money into the hospital, everyone loved him, patients, staff . . . '

'And you, did you love him? Is that why you took the blame?'

'No, Jack, not love, I know that now. Infatuation maybe, but afterwards I felt so hurt, so betrayed, I wanted to have nothing to do with medicine any more. I just hid away until dear Aunt Lucy jolted me into action. I felt everyone knew and condemned me, as a murderess.'

'That's ridiculous. If every doctor or nurse involved in medical litigation hid away there'd be no health service.'

'I know. It was stupid but it was so awful, being in court, the parents.'

She held her face in her hands. He took them and looked into her eyes.

'The past's over and done with. The future's all we're interested in.'

'I never wanted to be a doctor in the first place. My father insisted.'

Jack kissed her.

'No more medicine then?'

'No, though I can still use my healing skills. I'm going to be a famous herbalist with the most successful business on the internet. I shall cure and delight people with my vast range and knowledge of herbs. I shall learn to cook with herbs, I shall teach, I shall hold demonstrations here, go on afternoon television perhaps . . . '

'And do you think,' he murmured after a very long kiss, 'you could possibly add to that long list, farmer's wife? You must know I love you, Daisy, and a future without you would be too bleak even to contemplate.'

'I think I could manage that, given I love you, too.'

She kissed him back and thanked fate and Aunt Lucy for sending her to Elderflower Cottage to find such love and happiness.

Theirs was a Christmas wedding. Daisy married from Elderflower Cottage where she and Jack would live for a while. The entire village turned out to wish them well, Aunt Lucy could hardly contain her excitement and pleasure, and her parents were stunned by their daughter's transformation.

The Westons were severely out-numbered by the large, extended Hawksworth clan who had taken Daisy to their hearts instantly, only Helena remaining aloof, but Daisy's happiness was too great to be marred by a sulky Helena and a glowering Sonia.

'Besides,' as she said to Jack, 'Elderflower Cottage is lovely but it is rather small and maybe one day Helena can have it. High Ridge would be ideal for a large family. I was such a solitary, lonely child. I love your big family and I'd like to carry on the tradition.'

Tenderly he took her in her arms.

'Whatever makes you happy, and what I can guarantee is you'll never be lonely again.'

He sealed the promise with a kiss and Daisy knew she had truly come home and found peace of mind.